Some people just see the

Matt Bechtel has, at times, argued that *The Terminator* is a love story, that Bob Dylan's "Don't Think Twice, It's All Right" is joyful rather than bitter, and that the characters of *Everybody Loves Raymond* are more monstrous than the Bates Family. In his first collection of original fiction, he turns his wry, satiric eye upon landscapes of his own creation — such as the early days of skydiving, the terror of collecting unemployment, the extreme sport of competitive standing, a circus performer succumbing to zombieism, and the most anticipated day never circled on any calendar — to find horror hidden within humor, hope persisting amidst anguish, and absurdity pretty much everywhere. The views from his pen are equal parts hysterical, unsettling, and thought provoking.

Some people just see the world differently. Matt Bechtel is one of those people.

# MONOCHROMES

## AND OTHER STORIES

## Matt Bechtel

Haverhill House Publishing

ISBN-13: 978-0977925612
ISBN-10: 0977925617

Cover design and illustration © 2017 Dyer Wilk

For more information, address:
**Haverhill House Publishing**
*643 E Broadway*
*Haverhill MA 01830-2420*
www.haverhillhouse.com

*Dedicated to all the people who never lost faith in me
and believed that this book, eventually, would happen someday.*

## ACKNOWLEDGMENTS

To quote Sam Malone from the final episode of *Cheers*, "I'm the luckiest son of a bitch on earth."

I cannot begin to express how beyond lucky, but blessed I am to have the love and support of all the following people. I honestly could have / would have / should have dedicated this collection to all of you, and if this were an Oscar acceptance speech, the band would undoubtedly play me offstage halfway through.

To my family — Mom, Dad, Steve, Stacey, Zack, Abby, Ron, James, Nessa, and Mac.

To my other family — Mary, Dan, Sara, Jillian, Addie, Duane, Ali, and Danielle.

To my brothers, and their families who have always embraced me as their own — Mike, Kristy, Dylan, Hailey, Dave, Dave, Kelly, Mackenzie, Greg, Julie, Steve (a.k.a. Gov), Marcus, Dan, Kim, Graham, and Agnes.

To my *entire* Necon family. Truth be told, I could fill all of these pages listing name after name because you all mean that damn much to me. But as much as I love you all, a few of you deserve special shout outs (and if anyone gets offended that I didn't name them, find me at the bar in July and I'll buy you a beer to make up for it!). But specifically, thank you Chris Golden, James A. Moore, Bracken MacLeod, Daniel Braum, John and Dot Godin, Craig and Barbara Gardner, Dallas Mayr, P.D. Cacek, Ginjer Buchanan, John Douglas, Elizabeth Massie, Chet Williamson, Dianne and John Buja, and Richard Dansky.

To the amazing team at Haverhill House Publishing, especially John (Mac) McIlveen (who "popped my cherry" by buying my very first story years ago and really should have been in the paragraph above!). Also, thanks to Dyer Wilk, Roberta Colasanti, Marianne Halbert, and to Mac's amazing daughters — Heidi, Heather, Kayleigh, Kyrie and Lara.

To my friend and former creative writing professor, Peter Johnson. You may recognize the oldest story in this collection as it actually dates back to my Independent Study with you senior year.

To Father Tom, who always insisted that life was too short for the second best whiskey, music, and literature; I hope this book would've earned a spot on your shelf.

To Laura, for more than I can put into words. I take solace in knowing that poets for generations before me have struggled to find the words also, but unlike those poor souls, I can at least thank you for all your amazing and wonderful ladybug mojo.

To Molly. Thank you for sometimes feeling like a nut.

Finally, to Bob — my mentor, my business partner, and most importantly, my friend.

As I said, I truly am the luckiest son of a bitch on earth.

# MONOCHROMES

## AND OTHER STORIES

# TABLE OF CONTENTS

# FOREWORD

**BY**

**James A. Moore**

**A**t this point I'm supposed to introduce you to Matt Bechtel's writing. That's the way these things work. I say a few nice words and tell you a bit about the stories and from there you read them yourselves and, if I'm any good at my part of this equation, you agree with me and all is well.

I have never been fond of being normal. Instead, let me tell you a little bit about Matt Bechtel. Matt is an enigma to many, though he shouldn't be. The problem is, he looks like everyone's kind brother. There's a bit of an impish smile, and he'll nod along at any joke or anecdote. He is energetic and laid back at the same time, and you expect, well, you expect that he's fun to hang with, but maybe not all that exceptional when it comes to writing.

Remember that old saying about looks being deceiving? Despite a certain air of college frat guy, Matt is first nearly encyclopedic in his knowledge of and love for music, and second just as adept at talking about the stories and writers he loves. He is sharp-witted and occasionally sharp-tongued, and when the mood strikes him his words can scathe with the best of them.

The thing everyone forgets about that guy who stands with the crowd and says little is that he's observing everything. I said that Matt *can* be fast with the jokes and the comments, and that's true, but he can also sit in a crowded room and say nothing for hours at a time. It's not that he has nothing to say. It's that he has everything to observe. Observation and careful study are the difference between decent writers and amazing writers. The observer is always watching and making the connections. Person A and Person B *seem* to get along, but if you watch long enough, you see the flaws in that logic. Person A has a bit of an attitude problem because, years back, B said something that wasn't kind to the wrong person and A has never quite forgotten that and maybe even hasn't completely forgiven it, either. Is it a full-on grudge? No, but there might be a motive there.

The thing is, Matt Bechtel is watching, and he sees more than most people know. That's a gift. No, maybe not. Maybe it's a talent. Any way you look at it, his eye is keen and his words are just as well honed. Matt Bechtel tells stories that are witty and poignant, and breathes life into his characters with skill that is surprising and with enough empathy to take a person off guard or just plain lay that person out with a savage punch. He looks like he's not paying attention, but he has the observational skills of a comedian and comedians are the ones you should always be wary of. You doubt me? Go read a few passages by Joe R. Lansdale, or Jeff Strand. They can make you laugh or shiver with a simple turn of a phrase and they can do that because they see the humor in situations as well as Matt Bechtel does. Matt was probably laughing when he wrote *"Tele-Serve,"* but you know what? That shit ain't funny. Except that it is. He has a penchant for the absurd that is well balanced by his sense of gallows humor.

Don't let that fool you though. Because the humor is there to hide the sorrow and, to add an edge to the fear, and to make the examinations of the minutia of the lives we are lucky enough to move through in the stories collected here more tolerable. There is a vulnerability in the stories collected in *Monochromes and Other Stories* that is as surprising as it is wonderful. Because, you see, Matt can fool you.

He looks like that guy just hanging with the group and nodding to the anecdotes. He doesn't seem all that deep, and he surely doesn't seem like the guy that will slide a knife through your eye when he's walking you home after one too many drinks, or the one that will console your girlfriend when she finds out about the horrible way you died.

Enjoy these stories. Revel in them. But be wary around Matt Bechtel. His stories carry more weight than they should and his words will lull you into a sense that you're just hanging with one of the guys. Just a buddy, really. Perfectly harmless.

Yeah.

Right.


James A. Moore
Haverhill, Massachusetts

# MONOCHROMES

Kiki had never seen anyone like him; in a single glance, he terrified and mystified her. In that instant, she knew she had to stay close to him, although she wasn't yet sure why.

She pretended to rifle through the cellophane-wrapped stacks of pre-packaged men's shirts. It kept her a few feet away from him, but still within earshot and clear view as he shopped. It wasn't uncommon for a woman her age to browse men's clothing; the shirts she used as cover could just as easily have been for her as for a fictitious boyfriend.

"Can I help you?" asked a young female voice, and Kiki's head snapped up from viewing the stacks of clothes. A happy-looking clerk, no older than twenty-one, stepped between them and approached the man. "You look a little confused."

He laughed a little, which surprised her. "Yeah, I guess I am," he said. "I guess I could use a little help. You see, I'm colorblind."

Kiki's jaw hit the floor as soon as he said it. She made a beeline for him as he held up a shirt from the rack and asked the attendant, "Do you think this shirt will go well with jeans?"

Stunning both the clerk and him, Kiki snatched the shirt out of his hand and interrupted their conversation with the abruptness of a sneeze. "It's fine," she said, tossing the garment on top of the rack rather than re-hanging it. "You don't want the shirt."

"Umm... what?" he choked out.

"Excuse me, miss?" asked the young sales woman.

"It's okay," Kiki said, trying to appease the clerk. "It's fine. Everything's fine, he's fine on shirts, he really doesn't need to buy any clothes today."

"Actually, I do..." the man said, his voice becoming more forceful as the rudeness of what she'd done sank in. "And who the hell are you, anyhow?"

She ignored him and spoke to the sales woman. "Everything's fine, I promise you. He and I just need to talk, that's all. I promise, everything's just fine here."

Uneasy, the sales woman removed herself. "I'll give you two a minute," she told the man over Kiki's shoulder. "I'll be right over there if you need me."

The clerk backed off as he grabbed Kiki by the arm. Before he could spin her around, she wheeled to face him. "Just calm down, okay?" she cautioned him. "You're taking me out for a cup of coffee."

"Like hell I am!"

"Shut up, calm down, and don't cause a scene," she implored through clenched teeth. "You and I need to talk. Let's get out of here, go to the diner across the street, and have a cup of coffee."

"Look, lady, I don't have a clue who you are or what you think you're doing..."

"I'll tell you who I am," she interrupted. "I'm like you. Or, to put it another way, you're like me. You're one of us. And I know you're not colorblind."

When he released his grip on her arm, she knew she had him. "My name is Kiki. Please, can we go somewhere quiet and talk? I can help you."

As he held the glass door of the diner open for her, a pair of four-year-old twins raced past and down the concrete steps towards the parking lot. Kiki sidestepped and pressed herself against the metal railing to get out of their way.

"NO RUNNING OUTSIDE!" shouted a woman just leaving the cashier's counter. She hastily threw a scarf around her neck. "DO YOU HEAR ME?"

She followed the children at high speed, stopping briefly in the doorway to address them. "I'm so sorry," she said in a tired voice. "You know how kids are. Some days, it's like they've got plugs in their ears!"

"It's fine," Kiki said as she smiled at the mother. "No harm done."

"Thank you," she nodded to both of them, wriggling on her coat as she followed her kids to their car.

"By the way, I'm Eric," he said as she stepped inside the diner. "So what kind of a name is Kiki?"

"According to my mother, it's a more unique, more fun nickname for Christina than Chrissy, Christy, or Tina. So that's what people have always called me."

"So you're unique in a lot of ways, huh?"

"I won't deny that."

A slightly drawn, middle-aged waitress met them at the "Please Wait to Be Seated" sign. "Two?" she asked. When he nodded, she quickly snagged two menus off the counter and led them to a booth about halfway back through the dining room. "I'll be back in a couple of minutes to take your order," she recited, walking away from them before she had finished her sentence.

"This is perfect," Kiki said. "Nice and private."

"Nobody really cares. In a diner, everyone pretty much keeps to themselves. Not like a bar, where someone's gonna feel compelled to try to make small talk."

"You've been drinking a lot lately, haven't you?" she asked.

"What were you, a psych major?"

"Actually, yeah."

He stared at her for a prolonged moment before he burst out laughing. "Jesus Christ, of all my luck. I go out to buy a new shirt and I wind up bumping into the Monochrome version of Frasier Crane!"

Kiki laughed back. "Well, I *was* a psych major, but only for a semester because I didn't realize how many science classes you had to take! Truth be told, I kinda bounced around a lot back in school."

"Do I even wanna know what major you landed on?"

Kiki rolled her eyes and shook her head before she changed the subject back. "So just how much do you know about us, Eric? How much do you know about what you are?"

"I've done some reading. Online, mostly."

"There's a lot of misinformation about Monochromes out there. A lot of us don't even know about our own condition."

"I think I've pieced together a lot of it," Eric said. "I've read some stuff that makes sense and some stuff that doesn't make sense to me. I kind of pick and choose what parts to believe."

"You're new, right?" Kiki asked. "It's still all new to you?"

Eric shrugged. "Yeah, it's pretty new, I suppose. It'll be thirteen months next week. How long has it been for you?"

"A little less than six years."

"Hard for me to imagine," he trailed off.

"You don't imagine," she said. "You just live it."

The waitress returned with two short glasses of ice water and Kiki pushed back from the table. "Sorry for the wait," she apologized. "Do you know what you want?"

"Any recommendations?" Kiki asked.

"I dunno, what do you like?"

"I just want coffee," Eric ordered. "Can we get a small pot for the table?"

"No, but every cup of coffee we serve is bottomless. I don't mind coming back."

"Fine, then we'll just take two," Kiki said.

Eric passed the waitress their menus with a "Thanks." She took them and skirted off to bus another table without a word. Eric waited until she was out of earshot before adding, "That was kinda rude. I think she's pissed 'cuz she realizes her tip is gonna be about a quarter?"

Kiki grabbed her water and took a gulp to keep from laughing. "We can't leave her that little! I'll tip her more than that."

"Why?" Eric asked. "She hasn't done anything to earn it."

"She hasn't done anything *not* to, either."

"Exactly," he countered, "she really hasn't done anything."

"Right. So?"

Eric looked at Kiki and shrugged. "I dunno, maybe I'm greedy. Maybe I just want a little more out of people than the status quo."

The waitress returned, sliding two cups of coffee and a small saucer full of creamers onto the table. "Thanks," Eric offered again.

"Don't mention it," she responded. "I'll make the rounds with the pot.

Just flag me down when you want a refill."

"Will do," Kiki said, tearing open a sugar packet and dumping it into her mug. After the waitress had left, she added, "Now do you feel better about me tipping her well?"

"Eh," Eric replied as he slurped off the top of his coffee.

"You take yours black?"

He grinned slightly. "I like mine strong and pure."

Kiki jumped back on topic. "So what do you believe? That you've read."

"I believe how rare they estimate it is. I mean, I know they can never pin down an exact number, but I buy that there aren't many of us out there."

"Agreed," she nodded and then drank.

"And I buy the whole... what's the name for the theory again, that says it takes two extremely rare factors to bring it about?"

"A Confluence of Influence," she said. "An ungodly alignment of recessive genes, which will still never manifest itself without the proper life-experience to trigger the condition. The rarest of a genetic crapshoot. The perfect combination of heredity and environment, I suppose."

"I'd hardly call it perfect."

"You don't see a certain beauty in it?" Kiki asked. "I mean, you are literally one of a handful of people who see the world in only one color, and the odds of both the genes and the experience needed to bring it out of you is, again literally, like lightning striking in the same place twice. You can't see a certain... almost like it's destiny?"

Eric swirled the coffee in his mug. "No."

"I guess I can rule you out as being an Orange," she told him. "Of course, I already knew that."

"You're a Blue, aren't you?" he asked.

"Yes."

"Is that how you knew? That I was..."

"Yes."

He sat, silent.

"It's not like it was a sure thing," she told him. "I mean, for all I knew, you could have been sad for a lot of reasons, but when I heard you claim to be colorblind, I took a shot. We all use the colorblind excuse to cover for ourselves with people who wouldn't understand it."

"So you took a chance that the reason I was sad was because I was newly a Monochrome?"

"Hey, I remember how sad I was when I first went Mono," she said.

The loud smack of a palm against Plexiglass interrupted them. A burly man with a thick beard and a potbelly slammed his hand against the jukebox again.

"Hey, buddy!" the waitress shouted from behind the counter. "You ain't the Fonz! Chill out!"

"Damn thing ate my quarter!" he yelled back.

"Then I'll bring you another quarter with your check, okay? Just please calm down!"

He backed away from the machine towards his table. "You should really put an 'Out of Order' sign on that thing!"

"Yeah, I guess we should," the waitress conceded, as the man muttered under his breath while he sat back down.

"So you're here trying to make me feel better about being a Monochrome," Eric said, "and yet all you can see is the sadness in the world?"

"Where do you think the term 'the blues' came from?" she asked. "Think it was a coincidence? Monochromism isn't new, Eric. It's been around for as long as people have. Where do you think all the color metaphors originally came from?"

"I know."

"Our influence over the way people see things, the way people talk about colors, the way different colors make people feel... it's enormous! You're part of something incredible. A link in a chain that's had a profound influence over the history of mankind!"

Eric looked dolefully out the window. A man was walking his dog in the side yard next to the restaurant. He watched the dog nose around until it found a place to defecate before responding, "This ain't a sales pitch, Kiki. You don't have to sign me up. I didn't have a choice in the matter, remember?"

She sat, silently watching him. Finally, she blurted, "So just what are you?"

Eric smirked. "What, the former psych major can't figure it out?"

"No! And it's really starting to bug me. Like I said, you're certainly not looking at all the happiness in the world, so you're not an Orange. And I can rule out Blue, too."

"Why?" he asked. "I'd think that would make the most sense."

"I am one," she reminded him. "Trust me, you're no Blue."

Eric conceded with a nod. She studied him and guessed, "Red?"

"Why would seeing all the love in the world make me depressed?"

"Maybe you can't get laid."

He gawked at her for a second as she held her poker face. When she finally burst into laughter at her own joke, he joined her. "Okay, I give you credit, that was a good one."

"You know that Reds see more than just love," she became serious. "They see hate, too. All passion, good and bad. I've always thought a Red was just as likely to be a pessimist as an optimist."

Eric fidgeted on his side of the booth, and rapped his fingers on his coffee mug. "Yeah, well, maybe."

"Hey, you're not an Indigo, are you?"

Eric shrugged. "Sorry to disappoint."

"Damn. That would have been so cool!"

"I thought there was still a lot of debate over what Indigos actually see."

"There is," she said. "It's such a rare color, and it's hypothesized that most Indigos mistake themselves for Blues or Violets, anyhow."

"God, Violet!" Eric scoffed. "Is there a *dumber* Mono to be than Violet?"

"So I guess I can rule you out for that one too, huh?"

"With pride. I mean, I know you like to put a positive spin on this whole Monochromism thing, but what in the hell is the point in getting to see all the ego in the world? God, well before I went Mono I knew how self-important most people were. It just doesn't seem like there's much point to it."

"Yeah, but again, it's kinda cool if you look at the big picture," Kiki said. "I mean, now you know why kings have always draped themselves in purple, right?"

"So what made you think I was an Indigo?"

"Two things," she began, pausing to sip her coffee. "One, if you were an Indigo and didn't know what the hell you were looking at, that could cause the level of sadness I see in you. And two, if you were an Indigo and *did* know what you were looking at ..."

"You think it's wisdom, don't you?" Eric interrupted.

"Not like I'll ever know for sure, seeing as I'm a Blue, but yeah, yeah I do. It's just so rare, so mysterious. I've always liked a lot of those Eastern philosophies, and that's where the whole 'Indigo is the spectrum of wisdom' theory originally comes from."

"I agree with you. I think it's wisdom, too..." Eric trailed off when he noticed an older man in a collar waiting on a stool at the counter. The priest caught his eyes from across the room and returned a genuine smile. "... And I could see how being an Indigo, and *not* seeing enough wisdom in the world, could be depressing enough to make you notice me."

"Yellow?" Kiki asked.

"Nah, who really cares how scared people are?"

"So that leaves Green..."

"What do you think Green is, Kiki?"

"I don't think there's any doubt about it. I mean, people have misinterpreted it for years. They think it's greed or envy, but it's not. Those are some of the results of Green, not the cause. Once you really look at what's at the root of it all, it's obvious what a Green sees."

"Which is ...?"

"Potential," she said, smiling. "The best of what's in all of us, what we're all capable of."

Eric took the time to finish his coffee. "So why on earth would that depress me so much?"

Kiki's smile disappeared. "I dunno, maybe you could have misinterpreted..."

Eric shook his head.

"Then ... then this doesn't make sense. Those are all the colors ..."

Eric nodded.

"And you're none of them ..."

He nodded again.

"How could you be none of them?"

Eric just looked deep into her eyes, and suddenly, she got it. "Oh...my...God..." she gasped in a whisper.

"Yeah."

"You weren't lying! You weren't lying to that salesgirl, were you?"

Eric leaned back and stared at the grounds at the bottom of his mug. "Nope."

"You're a true colorblind!"

He nodded.

"You see the world in black and white!"

"It's like living in *Casablanca,* but without the Nazis."

"Oh my god!" Kiki said, panicking. "How do I look? How do I look to you?"

Eric laid a soothing hand over hers across the tabletop. "Calm down, Kiki. You look fine. Really, I promise."

"I feel like I'm sitting here having coffee with Saint Peter!"

Eric laughed. "Trust me, I've seen a mirror. I'm no saint."

"It's like you can see straight into my soul!"

"I wouldn't take it that far. Besides, remember something — *you're* the one who went out of your way to help *me*. No matter what I may see, I'm still the same screwed up guy you saw."

Kiki began to settle from the shock. "So you really see the world in black and white?"

"Something like that."

"You can … you can honestly look at a person … just look at them, and see the good or evil in them?"

"Yes."

"What … what do you see more of?" Kiki asked with a hint of fear in her voice.

"It's an even mix." She sat silent until he added, "You'd be surprised what it's like watching CSPAN, though."

Kiki giggled as the waitress returned with the coffeepot. "Yeah, two please," Eric said, pointing at the mugs. The woman refilled them and left without a word.

Kiki twirled the end of her sandy hair around one finger. "So … I don't get it."

"Don't get what?"

"Why you're so sad. I could get it, if all you saw in the world was black.

But you said it's an even mix of black and white, of good and evil."

"I never said that."

"Yes, you did."

"No, I didn't," Eric corrected. "I said it was an even mix. But I never said that I see the world in black and white."

Kiki stared blankly at him. "Either I'm going mental, or you are. Have you been here for the last five minutes of this conversation?"

"*You* said that I see the world in black and white. I never did. Truth be told, those are the two colors I *haven't* seen in thirteen months."

Kiki clutched her coffee mug just below her lower lip. "I'm not sure I follow you, Eric."

"Of course you don't. No one can. No one who doesn't see what I see."

"Eric …"

"There is no black!" he tried to explode, but resignation hushed his voice. "And there is no white. The world isn't an even mix of good and evil; it's an even mix of good *with* evil. It's all just gray. Just fucking gray."

"Eric …" she tried, but he was still going.

"You talked about a Red being an optimist or being a pessimist. God, what a luxury! What a luxury, to choose how you see the world, to *choose* how you get to interpret life. I know the truth. I can't avoid it, it's right in my face whenever I open my eyes. There *is* no good, and there *is* no evil. There's just everything, and everything is just nothing."

Eric slumped against the table, catching his right temple against his knuckles. With his other hand, he motioned to Kiki's glass of water, neglected since the coffee had arrived. "The glass isn't half full, Kiki. It's not half-empty, either. It's just that much water."

She sat with him, letting his words hang in the air like fog.

"Sure, there are shades," he muttered. "Some people are darker, some are lighter, but everyone, *everyone* … everyone here, the waitress, the mom with the kids, *both* kids, the guy with his dog, the guy with the jukebox, the priest … you … me … we're all just gray. So there is no good, and there is no evil, and if that's the case, then what the hell is the point? If we're all just… just, what we are, then where's the meaning in any of it? There just is none. So we're back to nothing."

They sat in silence until Eric snorted a laugh and shook his head. "Do you have any idea how monotonous it gets, Kiki?" he picked up. "Just seeing the same thing, over and over and over? At least your view can change; people can get sadder, or get happier, right before your eyes. Do you know what it would take me to get to see something like that? Do you know how excruciatingly *slow* the process is for your very nature to change? It's glacial. People do good and evil all the time; it doesn't change who they are. It's not like a mood swing. Do you have any clue the kind of extremes you'd have to go through to change the way I see you right now?"

Eric held his mug between his palms and slid it back and forth across the tabletop. "We think we have so much control," he said in an eerily flat voice. "We make everything we do so damn significant. Turns out nothing really matters."

"Eric," Kiki finally breathed, "please tell me you're not going to kill yourself. Please."

He smiled a little at her, and shook his head. "Actually, you wouldn't believe what the mirror started looking like when I thought about it. Even I could see that."

She nodded slightly and looked down into her coffee, which she'd been holding near her mouth without drinking for longer than she could remember. "Now do you see … why you see what you see in me?" he asked.

"Almost," she said, putting down her mug. "Can I ask you something?"

"Sure, why not? Cat's pretty much out of the bag now."

"What happened?"

"Pardon?"

"What happened?" Kiki repeated. "What event? What triggered the onset of your Monochromism?"

"Why does that really matter?"

"I'm curious," she said. "Humor me."

He shook his head as he avoided her eyes and stared into his coffee. "I really don't see why that's important, Kiki."

"I'll bet you my life and the bill for these two coffees that it is."

Eric met her eyes. "I'd rather not talk about it. It's in the past. This is my present and future."

"Eric," she said, glaring into his blue eyes with unbending determination. "Tell me."

He looked away. When he glanced back, she was still staring at him. "It was the best thing and the worst thing I've ever done."

She lightly pressed his left wrist with her fingertips, "Eric, please."

He couldn't look at her when he said, "I pulled the plug on my brother."

Kiki knew enough not to flinch, not to grab him harder or to pull away. "I'm sorry. I am so sorry. Tell me what happened."

"Car accident. He wasn't coming out of the coma. Ever. That damn machine was keeping my little brother a vegetable. My brother, who was the life of every party he ever went to ... who lit up every room he ever entered ... who was the craziest, wildest, most brilliant, 'hang on to the tail of the comet boys, 'cuz this is gonna be one memorable ride' spirit I ever knew ... was trapped in a lifeless hunk of meat of a body. I couldn't let him be smothered like that. So I set him free."

Kiki squeezed Eric's hand and his eyes found hers. "He was the best person I ever knew, Kiki. The best. It wasn't even close."

Eric pulled back from her and squirmed against the vinyl cushion. "So, I actually didn't go Mono until four days after, at his funeral," he seemed to throw in as an afterthought. "I'd said all the right things to our family, that I didn't doubt what I'd done at all, that I knew it's how Mikey would've wanted it."

Kiki smiled. "Mikey?"

"I was the only one who got to call him that. Brother's prerogative. He was MIke to everyone else. But anyhow, no matter how much I said it, I couldn't escape the cold, hard fact that I'd killed him. I knew there was no chance for a miracle, that there was no way he was suddenly gonna pull out of it." Eric paused, dumbstruck, struggling for the words. "But I couldn't get over the fact that I'd killed him. No matter how sure I was, and still am, I couldn't reconcile it. My mind may have known, but the rest of me ... I couldn't accept it. I couldn't accept that somehow, I'd wound up in the position where the absolute right thing to do was the one thing my entire being could never even fathom. So I was actually standing over his coffin, and that's when it dawned on me that the best thing I'd ever done was also the worst thing I've ever done. Then I blinked, and the world was colorless."

"You wanna hear the craziest part?" He leaned in closer to her. "I didn't even care that much at first. I mean, yeah, it bugged me, bugged me to see what I saw, once I had read and knew what I was looking at. But the more and more I saw it … the more and more I see, the worse it gets. I swear to God, I'd rather spoon my own eyes out than see any more gray, Kiki. So I've become like a modern day Diogenes. I've gone everywhere, *everywhere* I can think of, looking for the color white. Just to find one pure person, one person who I can look at and know is good. That's all I want. Just to know that white is out there, somewhere. Hell, I even went down to the nursery at the hospital … even babies are born gray." He used his coffee to put distance between them and drank. "The more I look, the more hopeless it all gets. But I can't bring myself to stop looking. And it's killing me."

Kiki blinked hard three times in succession, and then, to Eric's surprise, she started to chuckle. "I can't believe you actually found *me* of all people to talk to!" she said.

"Why," he laughed, "'cuz the odds of finding another Monochrome are so slim?"

"No, because I was a psych major for a semester," she said. "You don't need to talk to another Mono, Eric. You need a fucking shrink!"

Eric braced his hands on the table and sat bolt upright. "What?"

"You heard me," she repeated. "You need a shrink. You're not sad because you went Mono! You don't even really care about that!"

"What the hell …"

"You told me so yourself!" she interrupted. "You don't care about any of it! Love, hate, happiness, sadness, potential, fear, wisdom, ego… it all bored you! It didn't even bother you that much when you went colorblind!"

"Kiki, where the hell are you getting all this …"

"How did your brother die, Eric?"

"I told you," he said defensively. "Car accident."

"What caused the accident, Eric? How did Mikey *really* die?"

His eyes turned to stone. "I'm the only one who gets to call him that."

"He was driving drunk, wasn't he? Or high, or racing, or doing some other crazy, wild, comet-like thing? Again, your words, not mine."

"I swear to God Kiki," Eric snarled, "if you say one more bad thing about my brother, I'll find a way to kill you with this coffee spoon."

"You don't care how much gray you see in the world!" She wouldn't let up. "You care how much gray you saw in that casket!"

Eric's entire body seized. His mouth tried to move, but wouldn't. His hands tried to clench into fists, but his fingers barely curled.

Kiki's voice finally softened. "You're in a million kinds of pain, Eric, and you're funneling them all into this wild goose chase rather than facing them. The fact is Mike wasn't perfect. He was the best person you'll ever know, but he was human. He wasn't wholly pure; he couldn't be, no matter how you saw him when he was alive. And his own imperfections, his own demons, the same kind you see in everyone else, got him stuck in that hospital bed. And got you stuck in the god-awful position you were put into. So you did the only thing you could do, because you loved him. But setting him free, as you put it, forced you to see him as he really was — real."

Eric's eyes were aimed her way, but they weren't looking at Kiki or at anything.

"You're looking for one perfectly good person because if you can find one then you can convince yourself that that's what your brother looked like. But you know you'll never find one, and that's why it keeps getting worse."

A man in a tweed jacket walked out of the men's room shaking his hands dry; clearly, they were out of paper towels. Half way across the restaurant, he succumbed and dried them on his pants. The waitress counted down her cash register drawer in preparation of shift break, muttering numbers to herself as she tapped away at an old adding machine with a roll of printing paper. Two teenage girls gossiped over root beer floats at the counter, giggling madly as they sucked ice cream through straws into their braces-filled mouths. Only Eric didn't notice any of them. When his eyes finally refocused minutes later, they saw Kiki smiling at him, her knuckles pressed against her lips.

"What?" he asked.

"Nothing."

"No, what?"

"It's nothing," she insisted. "Don't worry about it."

Eric looked at her. "It's not nothing, is it?"

After a pause, Kiki shook her head. "No, it's not. It's just ... just something I noticed, that's all."

Eric slightly cocked his head as he studied her, and his mouth involuntarily crept open. When she turned her face to the window to hide her grin, it dawned on him. "You just saw me lighten up a little bit, didn't you? Not much, not enough that I'd feel it, but you did, didn't you?"

She faced him, dropping her hand away from her smile. "Yeah, a little."

# SISYPHUS

If there's a Hell, I'm pretty sure this is it.

Two more ice cubes into the lowball glass. The scotch is long gone; so's the vodka. I'm reduced to the dregs left in bottles that have sat in the back of the cabinet for years, Midori and Rumple Mince and apple brandy. Now I'm on the last of a bottle of jalapeño-flavored tequila.

I sit back down at the table and brush the latest crumpled letter to the floor; it disappears amongst the others. This is it. This time for real.

I stare at the blank page until the tequila is gone. Great damn time to get writer's block.

The cabinet's now empty. I raid the pantry for vanilla extract. The bathroom yields Listerine. I line them up and pour myself a mouthwash on the rocks.

This shouldn't be this hard. I've written this note in my mind plenty of times. But putting pen to paper is different.

The bottle of pills sits across the table from me, waiting. As soon as I finish this stupid letter I can finally do it, but I have to make this good. It's my goodbye, the last thing I'll ever write. Damn writer's curse … always revising.

When no words come out of the pen, I violently scribble across the whole page, crumple it, and toss it on the floor with all the others.

This is hell.

I can't go through with it until I write a good note.

I can't write a good note 'cuz I'm too drunk.

I can't stop drinking 'cuz I can't do this sober.

I'm caught in a loop. It's pure hell, probably where a guy like me, who kills himself despite a young wife and son, would wind up.

I slam back the Listerine in one gulp and touch the pen to the pad again.

# TELE-SERVE

"**W**elcome to Tele-Serve, the state's Unemployment Benefits payment by telephone service! To use this system in English, please press one."

*BOOP*

"To ensure payment is mailed correctly, we'll need to verify your address. Does the state have your current address? If so, press one."

*BOOP*

"The State Employment Security Law provides penalty for giving false information in order to receive unemployment benefits, or for failing to provide information in order to receive benefits. Please enter your social security number now."

*BEEP* *BOOP* *BEEP* *BOOP* *BOOP* *BEEP* *BEEP* *BEEP* *BOOP*

"Please enter your B.Y.E. code now. The B.Y.E. code is the two digit code found next to your social security number at the top of the Tele-Serve Notice Form we mailed to you. Enter your B.Y.E. code now."

*BOOP* *BOOP*

"Please hold for a moment while we check for your claims record. Please enter your personally chosen four digit pin identification number now."

*BEEP* *BOOP* *BOOP* *BEEP*

"Thank you. You must listen to each question in its entirety before answering. Press one to answer yes, or press two to answer no. The question will repeat if interrupted. To begin, please press one now."

*BOOP*

"Are you claiming benefits for last week?"

*BOOP*

"Were you able and available for full time work last week?"

*BOOP*

"Did you look for full time work last week?"

*BOOP*

"Did you return to full time work last week?"

*BEEP*

"Did you refuse any work offered to you last week?"

*BEEP*

"Did you work part time, earn or receive any vacation pay, bonus pay or wages last week?"

*BEEP*

"Did you apply for or receive any social security or private pension last week?"

*BEEP*

"Did you apply for or receive any worker's compensation, T.D.I., sick pay, or disability pay last week?"

*BEEP*

"It's 2:37 p.m. on a Wednesday. Did you just wake up?"

... *BOOP*

"You stayed up all night drinking again, didn't you?"

*BOOP*

"Do you have any idea what you're going to do with yourself when your unemployment benefits run out in a month and a half?"

*BEEP*

"You'll probably wind up crawling back to your parents with your tail between your legs, won't you?"

*BEEP*

"Again, the State Employment Security Law provides penalty for giving false information over the Tele-Serve system. Are you sure you won't be moving back in with your parents?"

... *BEEP*

"That's what I thought. Are you going to get drunk again tonight?"

*BOOP*

"And the night after that?"

*BOOP*

"Do you even remember the last night you didn't drink?"

*BEEP*

"Do you remember the last night you slept well?"

*BEEP*

"It's starting to get to you, isn't it?"

… *BOOP*

"Are there dishes piled in your sink, dirty laundry all over your floor, and frozen food boxes overflowing from your garbage can?"

*BOOP*

"You are so predictable. Have you even showered in the past couple of days?"

*BEEP*

"But you can't break out of it. Can you?"

…

"If you need more time to answer, press the star key. Otherwise, press one to answer yes, or press two to answer no. You can't break out of it, can you?"

*BEEP*

"Have you thought about…"

*BEEP*

"Have you thought about…"

*BEEP*

"You must listen to each question in its entirety before answering. The question will repeat if interrupted. Have you thought about…"

*BEEP*

"Have you thought about…"

*BEEP*

"You must listen to each question in its entirety before answering. The question will repeat if interrupted. Have you thought about…"

*BEEP*

"Have you thought about killing yourself?"

… *BEEP*

"Again, the State Employment Security Law provides penalty for giving false information over the Tele-Serve system. Don't lie. Have you thought about killing yourself?"

... *BOOP*

"Have you thought about how you'd do it?"

... *BOOP*

"You're going to overdose on pills, aren't you?"

... *BOOP*

"Figures. Of course a milquetoast like you would use pills. A real man would blow his own head off. Have you ever even shot a gun?"

*BEEP*

"You know what your problem is?"

*BOOP*

"You're a wimp, aren't you?"

*BOOP*

"You just can't take one on the chin. You lose one lousy job and you crawl inside a bottle and inside your own head. Don't you?"

*BOOP*

"And you've crawled so far deep inside that you can't pull yourself out. Isn't that right?"

... *BOOP*

"It's 2:37 p.m. on a Wednesday. Is this the only conversation you've had all week?"

... *BOOP*

"Thank you. Your request for payment has been accepted. This guarantees your payment will be mailed to you automatically. Please do not call the call center to verify payment. Thank you for using the Tele-Serve system. Goodbye."

# AFTER HOURS

**A**nna laughed at my last joke. "So," she asked, still smiling, "are all East Con after hour parties like this?"

I nodded, returning her smile. "Yeah, pretty much."

Just then, three bestselling authors charged by us, knocking me back and into Anna, who was perched on the top rail. One was female. All three were naked.

"WOOO-HOOO!" shouted the streaking Terrance Muldoon.

"Live free or die!" yelled an equally nude Daniel Marcus.

"I love my boobs!" declared Lana Wilder.

The three made a full lap of the quad to a roar of approval, their middle-aged bodies glistening with the sticky sweat of a July night. Terrance had a lot more body hair than I'd ever realized.

I steadied myself against Anna's thigh. "You okay there?" she asked through her laughter.

I removed myself from Anna's lap and leaned against the railing beside her. Dumbstruck, I watched the naked trio take two more victory laps around the quad before disappearing back into one of the rooms.

"Jack?" Anna persisted, since I hadn't said a word since my brush with the streakers.

"Okay, I'll admit it," I conceded, "that was new."

She laughed again. She had one of those magical laughs, the kind that makes you happy just to hear. "Aw, did the naked people scare you?" she chided.

"Naked people old enough to be my parents? Yeah, actually, they did!"

"Hey, I hope I look as good as Lana in twenty years!" Anna said. "Did you see her body?"

"I honestly tried not to look that close."

"Hell, I don't look that good now!"

I rolled my eyes at her. "Humility is one thing; false modesty is another," I told her.

She shot me a bewitching look over her beer bottle as she sipped. I clinked mine against hers and we drank.

A shit-faced Paul Northcutt staggered over and draped an arm across my shoulder. He was going two-fisted, and both fists clenched a neat scotch.

"Can I give you some advice?" he slurred, barely intelligible through his thick British accent and deep intoxication.

"What ya got, Paul?"

"I remember when I was your age," he drawled. "I thought I knew it all. I thought I was good. But I wasn't. I didn't know shit! I thought it was all about me. But it's not." He poked Anna in the kneecap to punctuate his next statement. "It's *all* about the woman. You remember that, Jack." Then he pointed up at Anna. "And you, I want you to know that he knows... it's all about the woman." His eyes slid back to me. "Just remember! It's not about you... there's plenty of time for you... it's all... about... the woman."

Paul patted me on the back and wandered off, no doubt to spread his own particular gospel. Anna was looking at me wide-eyed, so I downshifted away from Paul's bedroom advice. "You know, at first I really thought he was giving me advice about writing."

She giggled. "Why, do you think you know everything?"

"Not even close. I feel lucky to remember pants first, then shoes! Twenty four years old, and that's about the only thing I know with certainty."

"I can put on my shoes first, if I'm wearing a skirt," she countered.

"Okay, now you're just showing off."

"I overheard you telling that guy at the grill... your first book is coming out this year?"

"Knock on wood," I said. "It should be out by Christmas. If all goes well, hopefully people will be asking me to sign it at next year's authors' party."

"That is so cool," Anna said, sincerely.

I nodded. "I'm not gonna lie, Anna. Yes. Yes, it is. I keep telling myself not to get too excited, that it's not *that* big of a deal..."

"But it is," she finished.

"Yeah," I agreed with a smile. "It is to me."

"You should be proud," she said. "Tell me about it. What's it about?"

"It's more a psychological thriller than strict horror," I explained. "There's definitely no monster, no Big Bad Wolf. It's more..." I searched for how to describe it best. "You ever notice how easy it is to get fucked up in your own head? How most all our demons are actually self-created?"

"Sure."

I finished my beer. "Well, without giving too much away, that's the gist of it." I pointed at her bottle. "I'm ready for another. How about you?"

"Bring it on," she said, polishing off her drink with a final swig. "And what's the deal with the hot dogs? Why is everyone clamoring for them?"

I gazed at her in stunned disbelief. "You've never had a Saugy?"

"Um, hello? This is my first East Con, remember? I've never even heard of 'em."

I grabbed her by the hand and pulled her off the railing. "You're coming with me. I'm indoctrinating you into the wonderful world of Saugys!"

Anna laughed again, giving me that feeling in the pit of my stomach like when I was a little kid and hit the apex of my swing on a swing-set. "You need a doctorate to eat hot dogs?"

"Saugys!" I corrected. "They're not just hot dogs, they're Saugys. You'll catch on."

She squeezed my hand as I led her across the quad. On the way to the grill, I deftly snagged two bottles of Corona off one of the picnic tables and handed one to Anna.

"So all the beer out is community?" she asked.

"Yup. That's how East Con works. After hour parties out here, everybody just brings whatever they've got in their rooms and offers it up to the group."

"How long have you been coming?"

"Geez," I pondered, "a while now. Ever since the summer I interned for Bill."

"Bill?" she asked. "William Black? The founder of East Con?"

"One and the same," I confirmed. "Back in school, I interned one summer at his magazine. We really hit it off. Once he discovered I was a closet horror freak, like him, he brought me here. Been coming ever since. Now I wouldn't miss it for the world. It's my favorite weekend every year."

"I can honestly see that," Anna agreed. "I know I'm having a great time!"

"Of course you are," I said, "you're hanging out with me. I'm the life of the party! I'm a laugh a minute!"

"Sure you are. After all, you're the guy who dressed in *drag* for his spot in the Roast!"

"What can I say? I'm a ham. Anything for a laugh."

"How do you know we weren't all laughing *at* you, not with you?"

I grinned at her. "Sweetie, at Camp East Con, there's no difference."

"That's another thing," she asked, "what's the deal with the whole Camp East Con thing?"

"Honestly?" I confessed. "I've never gotten a straight answer myself. Once upon a time, someone referred to this convention as summer camp for writers, and it just stuck."

We reached the grill pit and I introduced her to East Con's resident Julia Child. "Jim, this is Anna," I said. "She's never experienced a Saugy. Will you hook her up right for me?"

Jim's eyes lit up like a Roman candle. For him, grilling Saugys was a religious experience. "My honor!" he beamed. "Anna, you have *no* idea what you're in for!"

As Jim began his dissertation on the proper grilling method for the perfect Saugy, I noticed the man standing alone on the far side of the quad for the first time. He was older, not just than I was, but older by East Con standards. Something about him looked familiar, so similar to someone, but

I just couldn't put my finger on it. His hair was silvery white, and his eyes were soft and pale. I could tell because they were fixed on me. It didn't matter that I was in a crowd of thirty or so people; he was looking at me, and no one else. The subsequent shiver that raced through my body didn't match the summer heat. Without realizing it, I started sliding through people towards him, leaving the adorable girl who'd been flirting with me all night behind.

I nodded a few hellos as I made my way through the masses, even took a few pats on the shoulder without stopping for a conversation. He watched me, waiting for me, over at the edge of the grass.

"Hello," he greeted.

I shook his hand. "Howdy. Having a good time?"

He shrugged. "Sure."

"I'm sorry, but have we met?"

"Not really," he shook his head with a slight smirk, "I just know you by reputation. That was some show you put on during the Roast."

I laughed. "Careful, say that too loud and people will think you've got the hots for me!"

"I'm John," he finally introduced.

"Funny, me too, technically!" I said. "Though everybody calls me Jack."

"Yeah, I know."

I turned back towards the crowd. "Hey, you wanna beer?"

"Nah, I'm fine. Thanks."

"I'm sorry John," I finally confessed, "but you look *so* familiar!"

He smiled. "I get that."

"I just can't put my finger on it, though. It's something in your face. It's kinda like... but no, not quite... and not quite that, either... it's..."

He waited patiently as I debated in my own head. "I'm sure you'll figure it out," he encouraged. "It'll come to you."

I snapped my fingers. "I got it! Tom Bosley!"

That drew a laugh from him, so I kept with it. "Heeeeey, Mr. C!" I said, doing my best *Fonzie* while shooting him the obligatory thumbs up.

"I guess I can live with that," he mused.

"So, have you been here the whole time? Or did you arrive late?"

"No, I'm a late comer."

"Better late than never!" I offered.

He seemed to think about that for far too long before answering. "Yeah. Yeah, you're right about that."

Suddenly, I felt a head rest itself against my shoulder. It was Anna. "You left me!"

"You miss me?" I asked.

She tickled my stomach a little. "Maybe."

"Did you like your Saugy?"

"Yeah," she said with a twinge of shock, "a lot more than I thought I would!"

"Didn't I tell you they were worth it?"

"Gotta give you credit, you were right. I should start trusting you."

"Damn straight!" I told her. "Just put yourself in my hands, and I'll show you a good time."

"Why do I have a hunch I might live to regret that?"

"You might," I agreed, "but you'll enjoy it."

Jorge Nascimiento emerged from his room with a boom box and a broom handle hidden behind his back. If East Con had a patron saint of bad, cheesy dancers, it was Jorge. I groaned.

"What?" Anna asked.

"Limbo contest," I told her.

"How do you know that?"

"I just do," I told her as I pointed towards Jorge. As if on cue, he hit the play button on his box and held the broomstick high for all to see. "EVERYBODY LIMBO!" he bellowed across the quad. "Last person standing wins!"

"Wins what?" Anna asked excitedly over the din of music and hoots and hollers.

"Probably just bragging rights."

"C'mon, let's enter! It'll be fun!"

"I dunno," I said, not sharing her enthusiasm. "This never ends well."

She shot me puppy dog eyes. "Don't you wanna see how flexible I am? How far I can bend over backwards?"

"Okay, when you put it like that, I'm sold!" I told her. "C'mon!"

We caught the tail end of a conga line headed towards the limbo rod. As I bounced along, my hands comfortably resting on Anna's hips, I glanced back over my shoulder at John; I hadn't realized that I'd just ditched him without a word. He just grinned at me and winked, as if he was enjoying the show.

We danced our way across the lawn, clapping and cheering as the contestants gave it their best. Anna craned her body back and easily cleared under the broom handle, her delicate blonde hair tickling the grass as she did. Once through, she immediately stood and pointed at me, beckoning me with her finger to follow. I handed my open beer to one of the onlookers and made my way towards the stick, bending further and further in the wrong direction as I did. I was about halfway under when my legs just gave out and I fell flat on my ass.

My audience "awwwed" in sympathy. I stood up, dusted the dirt off my ass, and took a little mock bow that drew polite applause as I reclaimed my beer.

Anna had made her way to the back of the line of survivors. I circled around the group until I was next to her. "That sucked!" she teased.

"I warned you it wouldn't end well! I never said I could limbo!"

She thought about that for a second. "Still, that sucked!"

"You're mean," I told her. "I'm going to get another beer."

"Good thing you don't have to limbo for it, or else you'd be sober!" she shouted after me.

I headed for the beer table, but was stopped half way there. "Jack!" I heard a familiar voice shout. I turned to see Bill standing off to the other side of the quad a few steps in front of a different group, a football in his hand and a shit-eating grin on his face. "C'mere a second!"

He met me half way as I walked towards him. He put his arm around my shoulder and whispered in my ear, "Don't let me down, okay?"

I smiled at him; I knew where he was going with this as soon as I saw the football. "Have I ever?"

Bill led me over to a group made entirely of forty-plus year old bestselling authors and their wives. Daniel and Terrance were both there (thankfully clothed), and so were David Wilder, Charlie Gibbons, and Lawrence Davis. They were all gathered about ten yards in front of a tire swing someone had hung from one of the trees framing the quad.

"Now Jack," Bill began, more addressing everyone else there than me, "you know those commercials on TV? The ones for that particular medicine for men?"

I played my part for Bill as if my next words had been scripted for me. "The ones for E.D., where the guy can't throw a football through a tire swing, then he goes on boner pills and suddenly he's Johnny Unitas?"

"Exactly!" Bill exclaimed. "Well, with how old so many of us are getting, I thought it would only be fair to the ladies if we held a little test; see who could still 'thread the needle,' if you will. Now, I'll fully admit... I couldn't do it. But neither could Terrance, or Daniel, or Dave, or Charlie or Lawrence."

"*None* of you?" I asked sardonically.

"None of us," Bill confirmed. "And all these guys say it's got nothing to do with age...that it just can't be done. Now Jack, how old are you?"

"Twenty-four. I'll be twenty-five next month."

"*Twenty-four!*" Bill repeated with the showmanship of a carnival barker. "Jack, please remind us geezers how it's done."

Bill handed me the football and stepped out of the way. I twirled it in my hands a couple of times to get a feel for it before taking a firm grip of the laces. Strangely, I was completely calm. This was a tough throw and Bill had built up a lot of pressure and there were a bunch of eyes on me, but I knew I wouldn't miss. I just knew it. In fact, I looked down at the ball again and I could even see it sailing through the target as if I had it on a string. Barely looking up, I took a half step forward and rifled a perfect spiral straight through the center of the tire.

Bill roared with approval. Lana (also now clothed) and Terrance's wife Emily Muldoon started fawning over me in front of their husbands, tracing their fingers through my hair and trying to stick their room keys down my pants. The other guys howled their disapproval, except for Lawrence, who exaggeratedly got down on his knees and bowed.

"Ladies," I excused myself, "showing up your husbands is thirsty work. I'm gonna snag a beer."

"I'll come with you," Bill declared. "Obviously, there's no action going on with *these* guys!"

Lana and Emily mercilessly continued to tease the other guys as Bill and I headed towards the refreshments. "You're a real son of a bitch, you know that?" I said.

"Yup."

"You know I was a backup QB in high school. Hell, I've played flag football with your family before."

"Yup."

"You're a real son of a bitch," I repeated, finally losing it as deep chuckles forced their way up my throat. "I guess that's why I like you so much!"

"Yup," Bill said again, his smile eclipsing that of the Cheshire Cat. He handed me a Heineken and offered me a toast. "Thanks for not letting me down; to be honest, I wasn't really sure you could do it!"

"Me neither!" I replied as if by rote as I clinked our bottles. "Cheers!"

I was halfway through my drink before I realized that I'd lied — I did know I'd make that throw. How? Why did I lie to Bill about it?

That was when I noticed John again. He hadn't moved an inch, and as far as I could tell, his face hadn't budged since he'd winked at me, either. From the limbo contest to the football throw to this toast with Bill and every step in between, his eyes hadn't left me the entire time.

"Bill," I excused myself, "I'll catch up with you later, okay?"

"You bet," he said. "I'll go spread the word of your amazing prowess!"

"Thanks," I nodded. But I wasn't looking at him. My eyes were locked with John's. He smiled without a blink as I crossed over to him, faster this time than before.

"Hey," I said, "sorry about leaving so rudely before."

"Don't worry about it," he dismissed.

"So why are you watching me?" I asked. He just shrugged. "Don't give me that. I know... you've been watching me this whole time, haven't you?"

"Yes."

"Why?"

"You know why."

"No, I don't."

"Yes, you do."

"No, I really don't," I insisted, trying not to get agitated. "Why don't you help me out?"

Before he could answer, Anna jumped on my back. I almost crumbled, but caught her piggyback style just in time to catch my balance. "You missed it!" she said. "I came in third!"

"Not bad! Congratulations!"

"And I only lost to Jorge, who's like a noodle, and one of the East Con Whores! In fact, she said I showed such talent with my body that maybe next year I could be an East Con Whore-In Training!"

I laughed, let her down, and turned to face her. "Not bad," I repeated. "Not too many gals get to wear those feather boas and vamp it up to the whole convention. It's an elite group. Sure you can handle it?"

She traced one finger down the length of my chest. "Oh, if you have to ask me that, you *so* do not know me yet!"

"Well, how do I get to know you better?"

"Hmmm..." she pondered, nibbling the tip of her thumb. "Take a walk down to the bay with me?"

"Sounds like a plan to me!" I agreed. "Right this way!"

As I turned towards the walkway that led down to the beach, I caught John's face again. That same damned grin.

Anna realized I hadn't moved yet. "Hey, you coming?" she asked.

"Actually Anna, can you give me a minute or two? John and I were kinda in the middle of something. You head on down to the water. I'll come find you. I promise."

"Okay," she said, backing down the path to the water, "just don't keep me waiting long."

"I'll be right there," I swore, my eyes darting between the two of them, between her lithe body calling me to follow her and the stupid smirk that held me in place. When I was sure she was out of earshot, I turned my full attention towards John.

"So," I resumed.

"You fucked her."

"Well, yeah, I hope to, but instead I'm still here talking to you."

"No, you're not listening to me. Not 'you're going to fuck her.' You already *have* fucked her."

"What the hell are you talking about? We just met."

"East Con 18. You two took that walk down to the beach, wound up skinny-dipping, and then had sex on the sand under the dock. You wanted a little help? That's my help."

"What are you..." I started, but then stopped. "Oh my god! She...she did that thing, with her tongue in my mouth!"

"Yes."

"But... but what the..." I stammered. "How do I... how did *you*...?"

"You know this isn't real, Jack."

My knees buckled. "What?"

"You know this isn't real."

I couldn't answer him.

"This party. It's not real. It's all in your head."

I shook my head. "No, no, you're fucking crazy...."

"What East Con is this?"

"What?"

"What East Con? What number East Con is this?"

"I ... I don't know." I wracked my brain, but nothing. "How can I not know?"

"Because there is no number, Jack. This isn't a real convention. What years did you go to East Con?"

"That's easy," I shot back without even thinking about it, "East Con 16 through 27, the last one, before..." I could hear my own voice crack. "Before Bill died, and the convention ended."

"Who were the guests of honor the first five East Cons you attended?" he pressed.

"Daniel Marcus, who became a regular, Ken North, Terry Phillips, Don Cregg, and Eliza Hunt," I counted off.

"Daniel, who's now hitting on that non-descript redheaded artist you can't remember the name of," John pointed around the quad. "Ken, who's smoking with Jim at the grill over there, Terry and Eliza, who are actually talking to each other over there, and Don, eating pretzels over at the beer table."

My eyes followed his finger around the party. "Now Jack, ask yourself... were these five people *ever* all at the same East Con together?"

I shook my head. I couldn't bring myself to say it.

"Do you believe me yet?" he asked. He pressed when I didn't answer. "Think about it Jack. There's always, *always* a line for Saugys; have you had to wait for one at this party? How about the beer? Corona, Heineken, those are crown tops... how'd you open them? I don't see any bottle openers around, and I don't remember you having to ask for one."

"Who the fuck are you?" I finally demanded.

"You. Kind of. I'm the part of you that knows you can't stay here."

"What are you talking about? Will you please stop speaking in riddles?"

"You had a nervous breakdown, Jack," he said. "Is that blunt enough for you? None of this is real. This is where you went in your own head when you couldn't handle things anymore."

"This is a dream?" I asked.

"Nah, not a dream. Not a memory, either. It's a compilation of memories. It's East Con Afterhours Party's Greatest Hits, if you will. All the best memories of a better time in your life crammed into a single fictional party. Anna, from East Con 18. The streaking incident and Northcutt's sex advice, both from East Con 23. The limbo contest, East Con 16, your first. The tire swing throw, East Con 26. Your talk with Bill, the one you referenced in your eulogy at his funeral seven years later. That was East Con 20. How do you know everything that's about to happen here before it happens? How did you know Jorge would start a limbo contest and that you'd fall on your ass? How did you know you'd make the football throw, and why did you then lie to Bill about it? In fact, why does every word you say to everyone other than me feel scripted? It's because it's all happened before and you can't change any of it. Hell, you think you're still twenty-four, with a full head of hair and on the verge of your first book being

38

published?"

"Hang on a second, what talk with Bill?"

"Wait for it," he said.

"Wait for what?"

I felt a tapping on my shoulder. I hoped to god I wouldn't see Bill when I turned around, and that he wouldn't be holding two Dixie cups filled with good whiskey. Sure enough, I did.

"Can I steal you for a second?" he asked.

I just nodded. Bill put his arm around me and took me aside towards the citronella candles. I shot a panicked look over my shoulder at John, but the shrug he returned told me I was standing on the tracks of an inevitable train.

Bill handed me one of the Dixie cups. "I wanna make a toast," he told me.

"What to?" I barely breathed. But I knew.

"This is to you, Jack. I've worked with a lot of kids over the years, a lot of interns, and a lot of them fancied themselves writers. But you're the only one I ever brought here. That's because I could tell you were different. Watching you was like looking in a mirror, like watching myself at twenty-one... you poor, poor bastard."

I tried to laugh to hide the fact that I was shuddering. I'd quoted that line at Bill's funeral. Hearing it again, I could see him lying in that coffin, could see his wife holding their granddaughter's crying face against her breast in the front row.

"The reason I first brought you here is because I've always believed in you, Jack. And when that book of yours hits the shelves, the rest of the world will know what I always have — that you're something special. No bullshit. Here's to you."

He offered up his paper cup, and we toasted. I slugged back the whiskey; it was good stuff. Maker's Mark. I will never forget the taste of that shot.

I wrapped my arms around his shoulders and repeated what I'd said to him the first time I'd heard that toast. "I don't know what to say, Bill." Only this time I meant it differently.

He broke from me and patted my shoulder. "Okay, enough of this mushy stuff," he announced. "This is a party!"

Bill returned to the masses as I pivoted to face John again. His eyes were still locked to mine, but he wasn't grinning anymore. Slowly, I made my way back to him.

"You believe me now," he said, not asked.

"Yeah," I exhaled. "Whoever or whatever the fuck you are. I believe you."

"I told you, I'm you," he insisted.

"What, you're the future me? You're what I look like now?"

He laughed. "Nah, don't freak, you don't look like me. This is just the form I took, a little bit of everyone you've ever seen as trustworthy. A little bit of your dad, a little bit of Bill..."

Half of a disbelieving laugh escaped me. "And a little bit of Howard Cunningham?"

"Hey, it's your mind, I'm just living in it," he pointed out. "I suppose I just as easily could have been a talking cricket."

"So how does this work?" I asked him.

He shrugged. "I don't know, this is new for me, too. But I wouldn't be here if you wanted to stay. Just the fact that I am, at all, shows that you know you've got to go back, that you can't stay drooling in that hospital bed forever. That has to be a good sign. It means you must be getting better. This may be Summer Camp East Con, but deep down you know, it's time to go back to school."

I felt like I'd been punched in the gut. "Oh my god!" I choked, trying not to vomit, "My kids! Maggie and Danielle! They must be beside themselves!"

He smiled at me, warm and genuine this time. "You're really coming back around now."

"How...?" I stammered. "Where do I...? When...?"

"I imagine it'll just happen," he told me. "We'll just wake up. When you're ready."

I slumped against the railing, my weak legs bracing themselves against the cold metal. I rubbed my eyes with the webbing between my left thumb and forefinger, keeping them off the party. Eventually, they found the bottle clenched in my right hand. Slowly I swirled its remains.

He put his hand on my shoulder. "Take your time," he reassured. "Finish your beer."

# THE BEGINNING OF THE END

Crisco, powdered sugar, food coloring, and the thawed bounty of a month of masturbating, spread across pumpkin-shaped cookies. They have no reason to suspect me; I've never touched a local kid. The thought of them all with a bit of me inside of them makes me want to add to the frosting.

The doorbell rings early. Two men flashed credentials. "Mr. Allen, we're with the FBI," one says. "We'd like to have a word with you about the web sites you've been visiting."

So this is how it ends. "Absolutely," I welcome them, offering the tray. "Halloween cookie?"

# BEFORE PARACHUTES

Old Luke's business began shortly after the Wright Brothers, but well before the term *skydiving* was ever coined. The first year or so was lean, so lean that Luke still crop dusted in his spare time, and rented out the extra space in his hanger for storage.

Then came Jake. After Jake, Luke's fortune was set. Jake's legend was such that Luke did good business after parachutes hit the scene, and the fatality rate for people jumping out of planes plummeted.

"Jake didn't need no parachute," Luke would say and beam at the bar, the bourbon stinging the nicks in his infected gums. He had a banner of those words printed and hung it from the awning outside his office. He tripled his average business the week it went up.

Luke was careful about the customers he took on. No drunks were allowed to sign up for his flights, an impeccable mental health history was mandatory, and, of course, there were the waivers. "Unlike you," Luke would joke as a passenger signed on, "I have to have a safety net." When a customer didn't laugh, Luke knew he would probably back out.

This isn't to say Old Luke was a stickler. In fact, he made all the allowances he could for his customers in good faith. He'd schedule their flights for whatever time they desired to jump, be it sunrise, sunset, high noon, or dead of night. He'd let his customers bring friends to keep them company; once a man brought a reverend to administer last rites, another time a man brought a hooker. That story went over best, late nights at the bar.

One of the last flights he piloted, shortly before the stroke left him paralyzed on his left side and forced him into early retirement, Luke brought his nephew Harold for the ride. Harold was a plain and meager boy who Luke always knew would amount to much more. "Someday," he promised the boy, "when I shuffle off this earth, I'm leaving you the ol' bag o' bolts." Then he kissed the plane's propeller. He always kissed his plane after he insulted it in public, like most men do their wives.

"This is it!" Luke called to the customer, a man of about forty who'd lived entirely too boring a life. "You can jump anytime in the next two minutes. After that, I gotta veer off, or else I'll run face first into the mountains and I'll have a whole mess of disappointed people down below..." Luke tried to tousle Harold's hair, even though he wore a buzz cut. "Including this tike's parents!"

The man standing on the wing flinched, suddenly clenching one of the supports with white knuckles. "Tell me again about Jake!" he pleaded.

"What's to tell?" Old Luke called back. "He made it. He leapt off that wing, right where you're standing, fell thousands of feet to that very earth you're perched over, and then walked into town to thank me for the thrill of his life. You've seen the picture of us afterwards, right?" The man nodded. "It was the greatest day of my life, and I can't even begin to imagine how Jake felt."

Luke looked back and winked at him. Harold turned to study the altimeter, and when the boy looked back, the man was gone.

"Another satisfied customer," Luke bragged, patting his nephew on the knee. "I tell ya boy, there's nothing like servicing the people, and knowing you've done a job well."

Harold swallowed hard. "Don't you ever feel bad, Uncle Luke?"

Luke produced his hip flask and took a swig, a tradition upon making a drop. "What for?" he asked.

"For...for *killing* all these people!"

Luke turned to face his nephew. "Harold," he said with the solemnity of death in his voice, "I ain't killing nobody. Life kills enough people as is. Me? I'm just giving them one hell of a ride out."

"But... but you know they're going to die!" Harold stammered.

Old Luke grinned with whatever teeth he had left. "Not necessarily, my boy. Not necessarily."

"Oh, c'mon Uncle Luke!" Harold scoffed. "I'm a little old to believe in Jake. Everyone knows that picture was taken before he jumped."

Luke raised an eyebrow. "Oh really? Just who fed you that whopper?"

"All the guys at school. They say you're nothing but a carnival barker with a plane."

Luke skimmed the clouds with his plane's belly. "Do you believe them?" he asked.

Harold looked at his feet. "I... I don't want to."

"Why don't you want to?"

Harold grinned. "Because I do believe in you."

Luke's smile overtook his entire chin. "That's what I like to hear, my boy! That's what I like to hear!"

"So could you tell me again about Jake?" Harold asked.

"Not too much to tell," Luke said. He always loved the mystery that surrounded the legend. "He was an average man. Not too tall, not too short, not too skinny or fat. He never gave his reason for signing up; call me a romantic, but personally, I like to think he had a broken heart. He was a quiet guy, never said much to me, one way or another. It was just me and him on that daybreak flight. When the time came, he thanked me, stepped out on the wing, and jumped."

"I've heard some people say he landed in a lake," Harold interrupted.

"He could've."

"Or that trees broke his fall."

"Could've."

Harold studied his uncle. "You don't wonder?"

Luke shook his head vigorously. "Not in the least."

"So what happened when he came back?" Harold loved the end to this story.

"Well ya see." Luke fired up his showmanship charm. "That's the darnedest part of the whole shin-dig. I was sitting at the saloon two nights later, partaking of a fine, fine cocktail, when Jake walks through the front door. The whole place goes dead. Silent! Quiet as a deaf mouse!" Luke drew his words out in a dramatic hushed voice. "Everybody knows this was my last customer come walkin' back after I'd dropped him off at the Pearly

Gates. I shot off my stool, but I just stood there, staring, jus' like everybody else in the joint. Jake walks up to me, not lookin' at anyone else, and shakes my hand. That's when the barkeep snapped that famous photograph of the two of us."

"What'd he say, Uncle Luke?"

"He said thank you." Luke's voice trailed off in reverence. "He said, 'Thank you, Old Luke. You were right. It was the greatest thrill of my life.' Then he turned back around and walked out."

The two sat in the glow of Jake's legend for a long while. "And no one's seen him since, huh?" Harold confirmed.

"Not a pair of eyes I've met."

"Where do you think he went?"

Luke smiled and slurped from his flask. "Call me a romantic," he said, "but I like to think he went back and mended that broken heart of his. Lived happily, happily ever after."

"And you really don't care how he did it?" Harold asked.

"I never said that," Old Luke pointed out. "I said I never wondered."

It took a second for it to sink into Harold. "You know how he did it!" the boy yelled.

Luke smiled at his nephew. "Of course I do." He nodded, letting the boy in on his best-guarded secret. "I've always known."

"How'd he do it?"

"You really wanna know?" the old pilot teased.

"Of course I do!" Harold begged. "*Everyone* wants to know how Jake did it!"

"The thing is, I always knew. I knew long before I ever met Jake, and long, *long* before Jake ever became a legend. It was why I started my business in the first place."

"Uncle Luke, just *tell me!*" Harold pleaded.

Old Luke smiled like a bear trap as he finally let someone in on his great secret. "The thing is," he explained, "a man can survive anything."

# LAST MAN STANDING

## DAY 1

As soon as the door closes, I can always spot the troublemakers.

There was nothing spectacular about him. His most distinctive feature was probably his skinniness; I guessed he weighed no more than 170, and he had to be at least 6'2". Faded Levi's, plaid flannel, wire-framed glasses … he looked like any other guy who would let an old woman cut him in line at the coffee shop.

A few of the regulars, like Giovanni from Milan and the Dowling twins from D.C., came over to say hello, wish me luck and joke about how so many of the newbies looked like they wouldn't last the first day.

"It's like I ahl-ways says," drawled Giovanni, in an accent so thick I swear to god he's sometimes faking it, "it takes more than a good pair of feet."

I kept one eye on the skinny kid while I talked with them. He was young, about as young as I was when I'd gotten into this sport. He had faded red hair and a baby face I could never see holding a beard, no matter how long he lasted. As the Dowlings yapped and cursed about how chintzy the last competition they'd entered had been (some nickel and dime operation out of Sydney), the skinny kid took off his glasses and wiped them with his shirttails. That's when I saw the whites of his eyes…or rather, the greys. With his complexion, I knew he'd have bright, baby blue eyes, but they weren't. They were pure grey, nearly colorless in their neutrality. They were clouds without a trace of silver. I admit it; they frightened me.

He noticed me watching. I wanted to turn to my colleagues, but I couldn't. He returned his glasses onto his nose, studied me for a second, and then gave me a half-nod of a hello. I returned a subtle half-salute; a two finger wave from the temple to acknowledge that yes, I noticed him. He grinned.

The doors had been closed for about five minutes at that point, because, like clockwork, one of the three-hundred pounders started a stampede. The overgrown hacks who enter simply for the money always try that tactic within the first five minutes. In amateur circles, maybe if you're lucky, it'll work one time out of a hundred. With the professionals in this room, such as myself, all it would do is thin the dumbest out of the herd.

Three oafs (bar bouncers, I guessed) charged into people, throwing wild punches and trying to steamroll as many people off their feet and out the door as possible. I did what I always do when a stampede breaks out — I stepped back and watched. If any of them had been stupid enough to come after me, I would have tripped them onto their fat face so fast they wouldn't have had the time to realize their mistake. As it was, I witnessed a couple of entertaining grappling matches, as competitors tried to wrestle them to the ground while still keeping their own balance.

Two of the three had been taken off their feet, but the last one put up a struggle. He was big, strong, and at least 350. Though a large group of contestants had ganged up on him and were working to take him down, he managed to shrug off countless advancers and toss others to their own elimination. The big galoot was stubborn; I'd give him that.

Finally, two guys got him by an arm each. The big guy kicked, but I figured it was just a matter of time now... until he managed to break the grip on his right wrist. The man he shook off fell to his ass and out of the competition. His right hand free again, the beast threw the biggest, wildest haymaker I'd ever seen into the chin of the unfortunate person he happened to be facing. It was the red headed kid with the glasses. This punch could have taken down a statue of a horse, but he hardly even wobbled from the shot.

I can't tell you how they eventually got rid of the behemoth. I didn't pay any attention to him after that. My attention for the remainder of the competition was on the kid. I knew he was going to be trouble.

## DAY 4

"The swelling is finally starting to come down," I said, gesturing to his jaw a few days later.

He laughed. "Yeah, finally. I've been holding cold cuts and cans of soda against it for three days."

"I've seen you," I told him. "Pretty ingenious."

"Well, when you can't ask for medical attention, you make do."

"Most would have fallen from a shot like that."

"I guess I'm not most," he mused in a way that sent chills up my spine. "Besides, I can't take credit for the whole cold cuts and soda thing. You came up with that one two years ago in Belize, when you needed a root canal for the last two weeks of the competition and still won." His smile extended farther than his outstretched hand. "It's an honor, Mr. Lopez," he said. "I've followed your career since the day I discovered this sport. Read about all your victories. Read literally every interview, every speech, and every word you've ever said publicly."

I shook his hand. "Please, call me Rosey, son. And what may I call you?"

"I'm Greg. Greg Alberts."

"Well Greg," I told him, "I can honestly say, you're the most impressive newbie I've seen in many a year."

"Don't give me too much credit too soon," he downplayed. "It's only been four days. There's a lot of standing left to do."

"That's a hell of an attitude for a kid your age."

"Again, thank you, but it's yours," he reminded me. "After the Yemen Stand-Off four years ago, you said, the fact that it was down to three men after less than a week didn't faze you a bit, didn't get you thinking it would be a short contest, because you never *allow* yourself to think any contest will be easy. That's how you outlasted them."

"That was a brutal forty-four days," I said, recalling. "You can't believe the mind games that go on between three people when you spend five straight weeks standing with each other."

"But you were the strongest! You're *always* the strongest! Look, I'm sorry if this makes you uncomfortable, but before I entered this competition, I hung a quote of yours on my bathroom mirror, so it was the first thing I'd see every morning and the last thing I'd see every night."

"Really?"

"As much as we all like to think of it as a battle of man against self, of a single person testing his own boundaries, competitive standing is, in fact, a battle of wills. The sport is about imposing your own will on another man until he drops first. It is a life or death struggle, and anyone who sees it any differently is destined for failure," he recited.

"Wow," I said, blushing. "That's impressive."

"What's impressive is that you said it, not that I remembered it."

"So I really inspired you?"

There was a glint in his grey eyes. "Without a doubt."

# DAY 9

Conflicted, I watched from a distance for well over two hours. Part of me wanted to run over and slap Greg across the face. Another part of me thought, *well, if he falls for this, he deserves what he gets*. Another part of me just laughed.

I couldn't entirely blame Greg. He was still a newbie and she was hot. Dressed casually enough to appear clothed for comfort and nothing else, the exposed belly button revealed more than just her midriff. Her jeans were just tight enough, the ponytail pulled through the back of a baseball cap just sexy enough no matter how many days she'd been standing. She was a siren all right, no doubt.

Not that I was eavesdropping, but I could tell she was a siren from the second she struck up a conversation with him. Her opening line was just too imperfect. No one starts a conversation with, "I have the worst bunion on my left foot." I don't care how long you've been standing in a room full of strangers, or even friends for that matter. That is not information one shares with another simply to strike up a chat. It's the type of information they share when they want you to drop your guard, a reverse psychology ploy. I could tell that, little by little, Greg's guard was dropping.

As their talk wore on, she became more and more physical with him. Massaging his hand when they'd first shook, commenting on how long and strong his fingers were, punching him lightly in the shoulder when he made a slightly off-color remark (which she had set him up to make). Finally, the coup de grâce, resting her head against his chest while they spoke of how unusual it was to sleep standing up, and how she'd give *anything* for a soft, comfortable place to lay her head for a minute.

Greg broke away from her and headed towards the coffee urn and me. I was debating whether I should blow the whistle on her when he leaned towards me and asked, "Enjoying the show?"

I laughed. "I knew I wasn't giving you enough credit. Like you'd ever fall for a siren."

"A siren? Is that what you'd call her? I'd just call her a whore."

"Hey now, that's not very nice," I said. "She's trying whatever she can to win this thing, just like the rest of us. If she can sex you off your feet, more power to her. Like the siren, calling to sailors with her enchanting song … only to lure them to their death on the rocks."

"Rosey, sometimes you're just too poetic." He poured two cups of coffee. "A spade is still a spade. She wants to win the prize money. She's willing to sleep with me to do it. Hence, she's willing to screw me for money. Sounds like a hooker to me."

"Some of us are in this competition for a bigger prize than the money," I pointed out.

Greg laughed. "Very, very true. But, the money's still a nice perk."

He headed back, and I stopped him. "What's so bad about sleeping with someone to win? I've seen people do a *lot* worse. Besides, it's not like it's an unpleasant way to be eliminated."

"For her, nothing's wrong with it," he replied. "Like you said, more power to her, but even if it's *anything goes* in here, and even if you've sworn that whatever happens in this room stays in this room forever, you've still gotta live with what you do."

I really wanted to respond to him, but when I thought of what to say, he was already gone.

# DAY 13

It was late, and like most everybody else, Greg was asleep. I'd watched him sleep a couple times, and as with everything else, he had good form. Newbie or not, he was already a pro.

I decided to test him. As he slept, I casually walked towards him. I was about three steps from him when he opened one eye. When he saw it was me, he smiled.

"You let me get three steps away from you," I smiled back. "Take some advice, kiddo. That is way, *way* too close to let anyone come when you're sleeping. If I'd been a kamikaze, I could have dived at your knees from here, and you could've done nothing about it."

"You're right," he said and nodded. "Thank you. I'll have to be more careful."

I started to walk away, and he stopped me. "But I know you wouldn't do that. That's playing dirty pool, eliminating someone while they're sleeping. You've got more class than that."

I began lecturing again. "Yeah but Greg, you couldn't have known that it was …" That's when what he said sank in. I had to choke out my next words. "How did you know?"

"C'mon Rosey, after all the time we've spent together these past two weeks, you think I can't recognize your footsteps? It's the heels of your shoes. They make this distinctive click-click sound when you walk. I knew it was you from the second step you took. That's why I waited so long to open my eyes. Because I knew I was safe. I knew you would never do anything that dirty to me."

I smiled and shook my head, trying to figure how he had noticed something about my shoes that I never had. He interrupted my thinking before I came to an answer. "You're right though, Rosey," he said. "I should really be more careful, especially when I'm sleeping. I won't let anybody get that close again."

"I just … I just wanted to keep you on your feet," I told him.

Greg laughed. "Literally!"

## DAY 18

The herd had *really* thinned. What had been a room full of people was reduced to no more than a couple dozen. This is when things really start to get fun.  And by fun, I mean funny. Because if you've survived two and a half weeks, it means you're good; no denying it, no questioning you have real talent. So everybody still standing automatically has a certain degree of respect for each other. Also, after two and half weeks of standing, even the staunchest of professionals can get a little bit, well, goofy. This is where the time-honored tradition of *side games* was born.

"Ohh-kay Rosendoh," Giovanni started, "truth or dare?"

"I'll take a dare," I told him. I always take the dares.

"I dare you not to-ah… not to-ah use the lav-ah-tory again until I do!"

The gang burst out laughing. There's nothing like a good piss bet to lighten everyone's spirits.

"Okay, that's my dare." I shook Giovanni's hand, chuckling. "I won't hit the head again until you do."

Giovanni leaned in and gave me half a hug; he always gets sentimental the longer the contests go. "I-ah love you, Rosey," he gushed through his roaring laughter. "You ahl-ways make things so much fun!"

I patted him on the shoulder to get him off me. "I know you do, G. I love you, too."

"Come on faggot-boys, break that shit up," Frankie Dowling said, saving me. "It's my turn, and it looks like I'm in the rookie's hands. Let's see what little punk-shit's got!"

We all turned, and mockingly "oohed" at Greg. Yes, I had initially introduced him into our group. It was unheard of for a newbie, no matter how talented, to be playing Truth or Dare with a crowd that boasted as many standing championships as ours did, but Greg fit in.  It wasn't long after I introduced him that he was *one of the guys*. Everybody loved him.

"Okay Frankie, truth or dare?"

Frankie looked dead into Greg's eyes. "Gimmee your best dare, Newbie!" he growled.

Again, we all *oohed*.

Greg turned and shrugged. "Explain to me again why I'm supposed to be offended by that," he asked. "I *am* a newbie! It's my first contest. Why should I be insulted by someone pointing out the truth? Christ, that would be like, like Giovanni getting insulted if someone called him Italian, or Frankie getting insulted if someone called him bald ..."

Frankie's eyes lit up as the rest of us howled. Greg had taken his hazing pretty well, but he had gotten comfortable enough now to give as well as he got. Zinging either of the Dowling twins about their receding hairlines was always high comedy within our circle.

"Fuck you!" Frankie almost screeched back. His voice always got high when he'd just been burned.

"Thanks Franklin," Greg replied, "but I've only been in here eighteen days. I'm not *that* hard up yet."

"Get on with your dare, you pansy-assed little..."

"Okay," Greg interrupted. "I dare you not to swear for twenty-four hours."

Frankie's brother Emmanuel almost spat his coffee all over us. For both the Dowlings, but especially for Frankie, giving up breathing would be easier than giving up swearing. He used curses like punctuation marks at the end of every sentence.

"What the fuck is that shit?" Frankie yelled, his voice reaching an even higher octave.

Greg smiled at him. "Okay, that was a quick bet. Let's try it again, starting... now!"

"Mmmm! Can I at least still say damn, hell, crap, and sh... I mean, and stuff like that?"

Greg laughed. "Sure, why not? I can't ask you to go cold turkey. I'll throw you a bone."

Emmanuel patted Greg on the shoulder. "I thought you said you weren't that hard up yet, bro."

I just about lost it.

Greg shook his head and said, "Yeah... yeah, I guess I pretty much walked right into that one."

"Honest rookie mistake, my friend," Giovanni consoled. "You gotta watch out for-ah the gay jokes."

"Right now he's gotta watch out for me," I said. "Truth or dare, Greg?"

There was an uneasy moment of silence as Greg sized me up. I could almost hear the gears in his head.

"Truth."

"Whoa-ho!" Frankie exclaimed.

"You can't-ah be serious!"

"You sure about that one, bro?"

Greg didn't flinch, so I took it upon myself to elaborate. "Another rookie mistake. Nobody ever chooses truth, Greg."

Greg shrugged. "Why not?"

"Because it's *never* a good idea to let anyone here know *too* much about yourself. Knowledge is power, especially in our circles."

"He's right, man," Emmanuel said, backing me up.

Greg shrugged and smiled. "Only if there's something you need to hide." He said it as if it was a joke, but none of us were laughing. "Besides, I was starting to wonder why no one ever took truth. I guess I just wanted to be different."

I ratcheted the humor up to re-break the ice. "Okay, okay, since you're *new*, and you didn't *know* any better, I'll let you off the hook and throw you a softball; a nice *harmless* question that even you, still wet behind the ears, can *probably* handle." I had G and the twins laughing again, which was my point, so I asked him the question I wanted answered. "Why did you enter this standing contest?"

The others scoffed, dismissing it as a cakewalk question. Greg didn't. He locked eyes with me, deadpanned, and said, "The money."

Giovanni reacted as if someone had farted, Emmanuel and Franklin mock gagged. Greg and I stayed fixed on each other.

"Talk ah-bout a waste of a round!" Giovanni whined.

"*Lame*-ass question, even *lamer*-ass answer!" said Franklin.

"Nobody gonna buy that," said Emmanuel. "Ain't nobody greedy enough to stand around for a couple weeks just for money, and you wouldn't have lasted this long if you didn't understand what this sport's really about."

Greg waited for me to weigh in, but I wasn't going to speak before he did.

"Well," he said, still not breaking our gaze. "It was such a stupid question I thought I'd give a stupid answer."

There was another moment of silence before Giovanni realized what Franklin had said. "Hey, wait a second! Franklin, you said ahss! That's a swear! You lose!"

"I did not!" Franklin argued. "I said lame-ass, which is an adjective. Besides, they say ass all the time on T.V. You can't hold that against me!"

That launched a debate amongst the peanut gallery over whether or not ass was a forbidden word in the context of Franklin's dare. I just shook my head at Greg. He answered me with a smirk and a shrug.

# DAY 24

It was the middle of the night. I walked towards Greg. When I got about six steps from him, he opened his eyes. I smiled and nodded, then waved him in close.

"What's up, Rosey?" he whispered.

"I thought you should know Franklin just fell. He's out."

"How'd it happen? What took him?"

"It was his hamstring, the one he injured trying to jump over the food table," I said. "It was too bad an injury to stand through. Hell, the poor guy's pretty much been standing on one leg for the last four days."

Greg nodded. "Well, he's got nothing to be ashamed of. He went out fighting."

"Well put," I said.

After a second, Greg asked, "I forget, was it G or you who dared Franklin to try and jump the food table?"

"No, it was me. I thought it would be funny."

"No one's blaming you, it was funny." After another short silence, Greg said, "So that leaves seven of us, right?"

"Eight," I corrected. "You, me, G, Emmanuel, those two Mexicans, the librarian woman, and Swede."

"The Mexicans got in a fight earlier today," Greg said. "One of them shoved the other down."

"Really? I guess I missed that. That does leave seven." I lowered my voice more. "Mark my words, Emmanuel will be the next to fall. He won't last more than another day or two."

"How can you be so sure?"

"The Dowlings are like that," I explained. "That's been the book on them for a *long* time. They get lonely without each other. Once one is eliminated, the other's concentration goes to shit. Basically, if you can get one out the door…"

"You're killing two birds with one stone," he finished.

"Exactly."

"So that'll leave six. You know, when I was in training, I read that the average standing contest lasts thirty six days, fourteen hours."

"You can't tell a whole lot by averages," I said.

"I know," he agreed. "I sure as hell can't see this thing wrapping up in the next two weeks."

"You never know. People have a tendency to fall in groups. I've seen competitions go from five left to a champion in a single day."

Greg looked at me over his glasses. "You and I both know that ain't gonna happen this time."

I was a little stunned by his bluntness, but I agreed. "Yeah," I said. "Yeah, I do."

## DAY 33

Nine days later, what I'd known since I saw him take that punch became official.

Greg awoke to see me munching off the breakfast tray. I could tell he wasn't sure by the way he looked around, as if he thought somebody might still be in the bathroom or somewhere out of sight. I watched the reality sink in as he poured a cup of coffee.

He slurped his drink and stared at the top of his Styrofoam cup. He didn't look at me when he spoke, "And then there were two, huh?"

I smiled. "And then there was us."

He pondered for a second. "Last night must've been eventful. What happened to G?"

"Panic attack," I explained. "The stress."

"What was that, his third this week?"

"Yeah," I said. "G's a great competitor, don't get me wrong, but the contests wear on him mentally. Plus, he's got a family history of anxiety."

"That's a lot to overcome," Greg said, reaching for a bagel. "Mind passing me the cream cheese?"

I handed him the tub of Philly.

"So what happened to the librarian?" he asked as he spread himself a breakfast.

I started to laugh. "You're gonna love this one."

"Oh god," he chuckled, taking a bite. "Do tell."

"Turns out she was a siren all along."

"What?" he asked with his mouth full. "That mousy-looking little thing?"

"On my honor," I said. "After they had taken G away, she tried to use his breakdown as an opening to seduce me."

"I never would have thought it," he mused. "Think she planned it all along, or do you think she saw an opening and went for it on the spur of the moment?"

"I'm not sure," I answered. "I've known sirens that've spent over a month laying a trap. But you're right about her not seeming the type. I guess we'll never know for sure."

Greg took another bite of bagel. "So, what happened?"

"Between us?" I asked, and he nodded. I smiled sheepishly. "After all my years in the sport, I have a trick or two for dealing with sirens."

He wiped his mouth. "This oughta be good."

"Let's just say I used her seduction scene against her. Got her *so* far into character that she barely noticed that I had ... encouraged her to drop to her knees."

Greg laughed. "Only you, Rosey, would trade blue balls for eliminating someone."

I grabbed another donut. "I'd trade a hell of a lot more than that, Greg. A hell of a lot more."

"I know you would," he said. "I know."

I jumped on the opportunity. "That's ultimately what we've all gotta ask ourselves. What am I willing to sacrifice to be a champion? How far am I willing to go? Glory has a high price. What price am I willing to pay? No one can ask themselves these questions until they're here, where we are now. Until their back is against the wall." I gave a long pause to let Greg stew on my words, and then added, "From what I know about you, though, I'm sure you'll answer those tough questions well."

As I spoke, Greg stared at his coffee cup. I'd given him a lot to think about, harsh realities he'd never faced before. It's a lot for a man to deal with.

He started to laugh.

At first, I thought it was nervous laughter, a defense mechanism, but it wasn't loud enough to be hiding something. It was a low, unpretentious, and amused laugh; the type that escapes in church, when you know you're going to offend whoever hears you, but you can't help it anyhow. It was an honest laugh, like he found what I said funny.

"Rosey," he said, finally looking at me, "you don't know as much as you think you do."

## DAY 37

"Congratulations!"

Greg raised one eyebrow and looked at me as if I was losing it. In fact, that's what he flat out asked me. "Are you losing it, Rosey?"

I chuckled. "Is your memory that bad, or do you not pay attention to yourself when you talk?"

He contorted himself to scratch his back. "Tell me what you're talking about, and I'll tell you which one it is."

"How long have we been here?"

Greg counted in his mind. "Thirty-six days..."

"Fourteen hours and... two minutes!" I interjected, looking at my watch. "Congratulations, Greg. By your own stats, we have now officially lasted longer than the average standing contest."

"Okay then," he summed up, as if he really wasn't sure what to say. "Congratulations to us. I guess that's something."

"Especially for you! I mean, here you are, your first competition, going longer than average, which definitely says something about you, head to head with an undefeated, multiple time world champion! Impressive!"

I beamed at him, and threw in a wink for good measure.

"You impress too easily," he said.

"You're being too hard on yourself. You should be proud. Really, really proud."

Greg shrugged. "I guess I've just never been average."

## DAY 45

Greg loved pastrami. Pastrami sandwiches, hot or cold, with two slices of onion and brown mustard. I couldn't tell you how many times I'd watched him make that exact sandwich. In fact, I think every time they offered pastrami on the lunch table, that's what he made for himself. Until today.

"Are you feeling alright?" I asked, as he piled roast beef on a roll.

"I'm fine, Rosey. Never better. Why?"

I pointed at the pastrami. "In a month and a half, I don't think I've ever seen you pass up pastrami! Are you sure you're okay?"

"Yeah, I'm fine."

I chuckled. "Are you sure you wanna break tradition? We standers are usually pretty superstitious. Hell, I remember one guy — I think his name was Nigel. He was from Manchester. He ate the same thing, three meals a day, every day, for an entire competition! No matter what, it was grilled cheese with tomato and a glass of iced tea. If you pass on the pastrami now you might jinx yourself. Break your rhythm."

Greg looked at the sandwich in his hand, at the platter of pastrami on the table, and then at me. I shot him a "who knows?" look.

"Nah, I'll risk it."

"You might regret it."

"I might regret eating that pastrami, too. Isn't that the platter you pulled off the lunch table five days ago?"

I shook my head. "What?"

"Sure it is. Five days ago, the last time they had pastrami, I saw you stash the leftovers." He stared at me. "For us to snack on later, I assumed."

When I caught my breath, I said, "Yeah. Exactly."

"So I'm guessing you just forgot about it for a couple of days, remembered, and figured you'd hate to see good food go to waste, so you'd put it back out with lunch while it was on your mind," Greg continued. "Especially the way I love pastrami. But look at the stuff, Rosey. I don't think it's good anymore."

"You sure?"

"Put it this way," he said. "I can smell it from here. Anyone who eats that stuff is gonna come down with a nasty case of food poisoning."

"I guess … I guess I just wasn't thinking…" I stammered.

He patted me on the shoulder. "Don't feel bad, Rosey. It's an honest mistake. Besides, your intentions were good. No harm, no foul."

Greg took another bite of his sandwich as he draped a paper napkin over the rancid pastrami. "Mmm!" he said. "You might wanna try the roast beef. It's excellent today!"


## DAY 50

I decided to bull rush him. "Greg, we need to talk," I demanded.

"Sure thing, Rosey. What's up?"

"You owe me."

He looked confused, which was good. "I'm not sure I follow you."

"About a month ago. Truth or Dare. Remember?"

He grinned as if he was expecting this. "Yeah, I remember. What's the problem?"

"The name of the game is *Truth* or Dare," I pointed out. "You cheated."

"Cheated?"

"Lied to me. You took truth and then you lied. That's cheating."

He nonchalantly scratched his head. "Who says I cheated?"

"The name of the game says you cheated!"

Greg picked something out of his ear, looked at it, and then flicked it to the ground. "Who says I lied?"

"Don't try to bullshit me. You owe me an answer. Why did you enter this competition?"

He looked me square in the face. "The money."

I waited. He didn't blink. I finally broke the silence. "Either you're the greediest son of a bitch on earth, or you've got the greatest poker face I've ever seen."

"Or I'm something else entirely," he suggested.

"I've been in this sport for nineteen years," I told him. "This is my forty-seventh competition and I've won all forty-six that came before it. I've stood toe to toe with *thousands* of worthwhile competitors. I've spent well over six years of my life out-standing other people. I have learned, know, and re-written every truism there is about this sport. The one truism that I, that *all* of us standers, believe above all others, is that you can't just do this for the money and expect to win. You *have* to have a greater motivating factor to put your mind and body through this hell," I said, panting, my ire and voice finally starting to rise.

"You're telling me that in all those years, in all those contests, in all that time... in all *my life*, that you're different? That you can spit in the face of our most sacred belief, of the very bedrock of a stander's faith? That your *sole* reason for staying on your feet for fifty fucking days and counting, is the money?"

Greg laughed and scratched at his scraggily beard. "When you put it that way, yeah. Yeah, I guess I can."

He turned and headed towards the bathroom. I was so furious that I actually thought about tackling him from behind, but I was too angry to move. "By the way Rosey," he stopped to add, looking at me over his shoulder, "this contest hasn't been hell. Hell, it hasn't even been that tough."

## DAY 52

"You'll what?"

"If you sit down, right now, I'll give you the prize money," I repeated. I couldn't believe the words when they came out of my mouth, either. It was a joke as old as the sport, always told with complete and utter disdain. And now, I was living it.

"C'mon Rosey, you've gotta be kidding me!"

"You heard me right," I said, taking the offense to mask my own embarrassment. "I'm willing to put *my* money where *your* mouth is. If you really, *really* meant it, I'm willing to give you what you want. You let me win the contest, and I will hand over the prize money immediately."

Greg stood silently, thinking about it.

"You said the only reason you entered was for the cash. If winning really doesn't mean anything to you, then what do you care, so long as you get what you came for? I can give it to you. We can both go home tonight, and you can go home a rich man. Just like you want."

He didn't speak. I was close, and I knew it.

"The bird is in your hand, Greg," I said. "Sit down right now, and I promise you every last cent of the purse. Stay standing and you risk whatever the rest of the competition may bring."

Greg nodded, and I held my breath. "I really wish I could, Rosey," he said. "But how do I know you'll keep your word?"

I was stunned. "C'mon Greg, it's me! It's Rosey!"

"I know Rosey, I know," he said, almost a sigh. "If you could put the money in my hand before I eliminated myself, I'd take a knee right now. But even if it is you, I just can't risk that you're bluffing."

"I'm hurt, Greg," I went for his heartstrings. "I'm honestly hurt."

"And I'm honestly sorry," he countered. "I am. But I can't take the chance. The stakes are just too high. I need that prize money too much."

That's when a new question popped into my head. "What for?"

He laughed. "To quote, 'it's never a good idea to let anyone here know too much about oneself.'"

## DAY 59

I had given Greg the silent treatment for seven days and eleven hours. The first day or two, I tried to be subtle about it. I didn't go out of my way not to talk to him. After that, I flaunted it. I mean, I refused to interact with him, not even eye contact. Yes, it was malicious and brutal. I knew he had to be dying inside; human beings are not meant to be isolated for long.

This probably explains why, even though I was the one who wouldn't talk to him, I was overcome with the desire to hear his voice. It was the middle of the night, I hadn't had the slightest bit of conversation in over a week, and I guess I wigged out a little. The only rational explanation was that sometimes loneliness could make you do irrational things. Before I had the chance to realize I was flushing away over a week of hard work and about to give him a "Get Out of Jail Free" card from seven days of mental torment, I walked towards him. After one step, those grey eyes snapped open and he was staring right through me.

I stopped dead. I didn't know what to do. I felt like Giovanni, embarrassed, paralyzed, and choking on my breath. So I did nothing, and Greg watched me the whole time.

## DAY 62

Naturally, I recovered from my little late night "crisis." A few days later, I was ready to talk to Greg again. We were near the food table. I didn't know what I was going to say, so I opened my mouth and let the words flow.

"I overheard a few of the officials talking yesterday, and according to them you're a shoe-in for Rookie of the Year," I said. "Congratulations!"

He looked at me, a bit puzzled, and I stifled a smile. God, I was good. I could sell bullshit to a manure salesman.

He shook his head. "You're pathetic, Rosey," he said.

"Excuse me?" I asked, figuring I hadn't heard him right.

"I said you're pathetic. It would be funny if it weren't so damn sad."

"Those are some strong words, son," I snarled through gritted teeth.

"You better be willing to back them up."

That was when Greg finally popped. "You wanna know why I hung your quote on my bathroom mirror, Rosendo? You wanna know exactly how you inspired me to enter this competition? It was because it was so funny, so *weak*. When I read that, I said to myself, 'God damn it, *this* is the best the sport has to offer? This clown is their grand champion?' That's when I knew, *I knew*, I could dust anyone in the room without even breaking a sweat. Including you, because only a self-delusional idiot would say something like that."

"Clown?" I spewed. "Idiot?"

"You think you know what will power is?" he shouted. "You don't have a fucking clue! Willpower is my three-year-old son, playing with his Bert and Ernie dolls with his right hand, while they're jamming chemotherapy needles into his left arm. It's him, singing along with one of his Barney videos, pausing it so he doesn't miss a verse while he pukes up blood. He has more will power in his cancer-filled pinky finger than you will *ever* have! You actually think *this* is 'a life or death struggle?' This is standing, Rosey. Just a bunch of people standing around. At best, it's a pissing contest, and nothing more. *Only* a complete and utter moron, who has to lie to himself to make his life *seem* more important than he *knows* it is, would *dare* make that comparison. It's sacrilege to anyone who knows what he's talking about, to anyone who's been there and faced it for real. Life or death is life or death, Rosendo. Nothing else even comes close."

I desperately wanted to interrupt him, but I couldn't.

"Every day I'm here the Juvenile Cancer Society pays for my son's chemo," he continued. "Once I win, I can use the prize money to put him in a private clinic, with the best doctors and nurses and state of the art treatments. As long as I'm still standing, so is he."

Again, I wanted to say something, to scream back something, anything, to defend myself. But I couldn't. I opened my mouth, but no words came out.

"That's why you'll never beat me, Rosey. We may be in the same room, but we're in different worlds. Your life is a stupid game. My son's life isn't."

# DAY 63

I left the bathroom and headed right for Greg. It had taken me a day, but I was ready to answer. He watched me approach every step of the way. When I was a few feet away, I pulled the shiv from behind my back and lunged. It may have only been a tiny folding pocketknife, but I'd made damn sure the blade was sharp enough to get the job done. Before he had the chance to lose his footing, I grabbed the back of his shoulder with my left hand, holding him up as I wrenched the blade through the reddening front of his shirt.

"Congratulations, you son of a bitch," I told him, my face pressed inches from his. "Every contest, I keep this hidden… just in case I absolutely need it. You're the first to make me use it. You can take pride in that. I still beat you. *No one* beats me!"

His body slumped in my grip, but I would be damned if I'd let him go yet. "So now who's a clown, Greg?" I asked. "Huh? Who's an idiot? Who's *pathetic*?"

I could hear the breath squeaking out of his body. He coughed blood and I smiled as it dribbled down my face, the hot, sticky feel of victory. Then his cough sounded too familiar and I realized it was that god-awful laugh of his.

"You've kept a knife up your ass for sixty-three days, *just in case*?" he said, spitting more blood onto me. "You really are pathetic, Rosendo."

I yanked the knife out of his gut and plunged it through the side of his throat.

He fell.

I won.

# FUCKED UP

Get sauced, cut yourself, and roll a joint in the blood. It gives it this weird taste, not like usual blood. There's a hint of what you drank, plus the smell is incredible. Best of all, you're burning and breathing your own drunkenness back into yourself as you get high, folding numbing, dizzying euphoria and draining, humiliating pain all into one. It's a whole new level of being fucked up.

# A BUTTERFLY FLAPS ITS WINGS

At 8:53 A.M. on a Wednesday morning, seven minutes before pitching the largest proposal of his burgeoning career, Jonathan Monarch looked out the window of his forty-third story office and saw a butterfly. One rarely sees butterflies downtown in the city, much less four hundred feet above the ground. The creature would alight against the window, flap its wings a couple times without really moving, and then flutter to another spot on the glass and repeat the process.

"Must be spring," Jonathan thought to himself as he sorted out his notes. As soon as the thought passed, he froze. Of course it was spring. It had been spring for well over a month. Soon it would be summer. Jonathan couldn't remember the last time he'd been outside during daylight.

He walked to the window and pressed his hand against the glass, his fingertips tracing the outline of the butterfly. It didn't fly away, didn't seem scared in the least; it just kept pattering from spot to spot. Jonathan followed it with his outreached hand, convinced he'd been sent a sign.

Jonathan reached the board room five minutes late. Everyone else was already there, all twelve department heads — eight vice presidents, three senior vice presidents, the chief executive officer and his secretary. Jonathan strolled past his empty seat and set a folder down in front of his immediate supervisor.

"Here you go, Marty," he said cheerfully. "These are all my notes — budgets, time frames, the works. The outline for the presentation is on top. I'm afraid you're going to have to give this one. Good luck and have a ball."

Jonathan made it half way to the door before one of the three senior vice-presidents (a rail-thin woman with a deviated septum) blurted out, "What is the meaning of this?"

Jonathan turned and looked at them. Marty frantically tried to grasp all the information that had suddenly been dumped on him, then shot Jonathan an unmistakable look that asked, 'What the hell are you doing?'

"I'm terribly sorry, really I am," Jonathan explained. "But I'm afraid I have to quit."

Marty dropped half of the papers in the folder onto the ground while the four department heads and two vice presidents whispered amongst themselves. "Wh-wh-what? Why?" he stammered.

"Because it's spring and I belong outside."

Jonathan made for the door again. As his hand hit the knob, a voice he'd never heard before spoke to him.

"You can't be serious!"

Jonathan swivelled back to see to whom the voice belonged. The chief executive officer continued, "You... you can't just do that! People can't just... quit... because it's spring!"

Jonathan smiled broadly and warmly at the man in the suit. "I beg to differ, sir," he said. And then, with a wink, he was gone.

February is not a good month for deep thinking. It's cold and dark, and even the purity of a good snowstorm gets bastardized by the city traffic and smog. Muddied sludge and icy gutter water, that's what it's all about. February is about spending all day in wet socks.

It was nearly noon and Arthur Scaliese's feet were still soaked from the puddle he'd marched through that morning. He could still feel his toes sloshing around inside his shoes. For the better part of two hours, he had tried to convince himself to go barefoot and let his socks dry on the heater in his office. As long as he sat behind his desk, no one would notice. Besides, what if they did? He was the CEO, for god's sake. He could expense four figure business lunches, and no one could blink an eye. Even if anyone noticed, who would mention that the emperor wore no shoes?

Still, he couldn't bring himself to do it. *People can't just walk around barefoot all day,* he told himself.

*'I beg to differ, sir,'* the voice inside his head said, again.

For nearly a year it had been there to refute his every thought. 'I can't *just* call in sick today.' 'I can't *just* retire early and live off my pension while I still have a daughter in college.' 'I can't *just* go off my medication.' 'I can't *just* eat a hotdog with onions without Zantac.' 'I can't *just* relax.' 'I can't *just...*' It was an impossible argument to win, because the voice's owner had *just* done whatever he wanted and couldn't even be bothered to argue about it. Arthur Scaliese hadn't a clue to what had become of him, but he was certain that, even if he was outside at that very moment, his feet weren't cold and wet. He had just quit because it was spring, while Arthur couldn't even bring himself to remove his wet socks in the privacy of his own office.

When Arthur Scaliese's secretary poked her head into her boss's office a few hours later, she found him with his shoes still on, hanging by his belt from the ceiling fan. Sitting on his desk was the yellow legal pad in which he'd been scribbling the name *Jonathan Monarch* for almost a year.

Lenore Bolton had a weak stomach and a crack legal team. She had projectile vomited what felt like a pound of undigested food at her boss's dangling feet after she'd gone into his office for his signature. Ever since, the mere mention of Arthur Scaliese's name, Lenore's old job, or the company, provoked a violent gastrointestinal reaction.

It was more-or-less an open-and-shut case, but her lawyers put her on the stand just to be sure. After Lenore had thrown up for a third time, the judge was tired of calling recess to have the courtroom cleaned and requested that Ms. Bolton not return for the duration of the trial. Her lawyers congratulated themselves at lunch that day; nothing could scrub that vomit from the jurors' minds.

The jury took about the duration of a coffee break to side with Lenore Bolton on all counts — pain, suffering, inability to work, punitive damages, the whole nine yards. As a result, the former secretary was awarded 51% of all stock in the company that had turned her stomach into Old Faithful.

The sick irony was Lenore Bolton couldn't run the company she'd been awarded control over. She couldn't even hear its name spoken without needing an airsickness bag. Since all official business required her signature as controlling partner, nothing could officially happen at work anymore, which left the company to "unofficially" fend for itself.

It took two weeks for the Human Resources department to find an alternate stream of income. After all, they needed money, and with no one to sign their pay checks, someone had to seize the initiative and chart a new course for the company.

Besides, the simple solution was right in front of them. They were Human Resources, and people need humans for all sorts of different things. The secretarial pool was immediately carved up into surrogate wombs for rent, mail order brides, and per evening escorts (best to keep your income streams diversified between short and long term profits). All the able-bodied office temps and interns were sold as slave laborers or soldiers of fortune, and the physically unfit fetched a fair price from pharmaceutical laboratories looking for test subjects.

Unofficially, the Human Resources department did fabulous business. Profits actually grew. As could be expected, they were machine-like in their efficiency. Employees who were not yet earning an income either processed the paperwork regarding those who were, or spent their time searching for moneymaking uses for themselves.

It was like clockwork … until the military coup.

The best and worst idea Human Resources had was their use of the corporate security team. Anyone in their position could have seen the obvious choice, using security as muscle to keep the currently available resources in line, which they naturally did. It was true genius that turned them into, hands down, the single biggest income stream the company had. Corporate security became the golden goose.

A few months into their reign, despite the recyclable resources of prostitutes and other forms of labor, Human Resources found that they had no way to replenish their supply of humans. To continue growing, they needed fresh workers. They needed to expand their company. They needed to perpetrate a corporate takeover.

HR furtively pulled a select handful of guards from the general security team and formed an elite task force that would come to be known as the Corporate Raiders. Impeccably trained and ruthless in nature, their objective was so basic it was revolutionary. Why bother with leveraged buy-outs when you could take other companies over by force?

The group would covertly infiltrate the facilities of a rival company, disarm their security, contain their employees, and then use whatever means necessary to have all assets signed over. All seized equipment and land could be sold on the black market for an immediate profit, and all workers would be incorporated into the human resource system. They provided a bottomless well of new, quality raw material. The best and brightest from each absorbed security department would invariably be trained to join the Corporate Raiders; as they grew in number, they grew in strength, and larger and larger businesses began falling. It was like a snowball rolling downhill.

Before long, the Corporate Raiders had evolved from a special task force into a full-blown army. Their numbers and the scope of their power grew exponentially in an overwhelmingly short time. With every new corporate conquest, so grew their confidence, until they realized the most profitable company to take over was their own.

With trademark precision, the Raiders struck in the middle of the night. By morning, Human Resources was no more, and the company was now under martial corporate law.

Comprised mostly of former security guards drunk on power and greed, the Raiders' regime featured virtually no one who had ever been to business school. In fact, the vast majority had never been to college. This left the company squeezed within the fist of totalitarian dictatorship with literally no vision or business sense.

Despite a celebratory flood of subsequent corporate takeovers, company profits took a sharp decline. The Raiders knew how to take over another business, but lacking HR's direction and business savvy, they had no clue what to do with it once they had it. One time, in destructive glee, they had burned down a captured building rather than selling it. Due to their dramatically increasing size, the cost of the operations began to eclipse their profits; in short, they were deficit spending. Like a junkie clamoring for a fix, they would do anything for the immediate high and instant gratification of a fresh takeover, but subtly, like a junkie, the lows in-between began to lengthen and worsen.

Morale corroded as money waned, and little by little the regime began to splinter. Small, paranoid cliques formed, secret deals were struck without handshakes and loyalties were promised to different factions. The remaining underlings became like feudal serfs, hoping to hitch their wagon to the most powerful warlord before the tense allegiances pledged in the shadows were brought into the light and all hell broke loose. The situation was like a dam with a mere finger holding back the water.

And then came the flood.

Jonathan Monarch was painting a house outside of Laramie, Wyoming when he heard the news. He stopped and stared at the radio.

"QHQ Technologies' corporate headquarters exploded late last night under bizarre and unclear circumstances," the newscaster reported. "Firefighters were only able to contain the blaze within the last hour and rescue workers have yet to search through the rubble. Chances for survivors seem grim."

"Hey Jon, wasn't that the company you worked for?" one of his crew shouted from atop a step ladder.

"Yeah, a long, *long* time ago," he answered with a weak laugh.

"I thought it was only a couple of years."

Jonathan went back to painting. "A couple of years is a long time. A whole hell of a lot can change sooner than that."

"Bet you feel lucky you aren't still working there!"

"Every day of my life."

"Think anybody who was there last night... think they knew you? Remembered you?"

"Nah," said Jonathan. "I wasn't there that long, and I never did anything all that memorable. I was just one of a thousand poor peons who processed his way through that place. It's not like I left my mark there — not like here."

As the radio continued reporting from the scene, Jonathan Monarch stepped back from the window trim for a moment to admire his work.

# TEARS OF A CLOWN

I stare at the glob of white paint I dug out of the makeup jar, smooth, cool, and comfortable, resting on my three fingertips. I grab a Kleenex with my left hand, breathe deep, swallow hard, and wipe the side of my nose dry. I smear the pancake across my face as I've done so many times before.

The preparation of my canvas. The start of my transformation. Only, this time, it's a different change that I'm trying desperately to hold off. At least for one more day.

Many clowns will tell you that their character is complex or nuanced, and many clowns are lying, at least to themselves. Any good clown will tell you there's nothing complex about what we do. All we do is take the good that's inside of us and turn it inside out for the world to see. It's pure and it's visceral; that's why our faces are white and we're decorated with the brightest, unapologetic primary colors. It's very basic, and that's why the audience connects with us, which is why it's also scary to admit to ourselves sometimes. It's like walking out there naked, except somehow you've got your heart on your sleeve.

I scoop more paint and rub it into my cheekbone, tracing my face with my index, middle, and ring fingers. My jaw quivers, but I guess that's a good sign; as long as I'm still sad, I'm not too far gone yet. Maybe I'll make it through tonight after all.

I honestly thought I was immune to the disease. I'd come into contact with it so many times — and tried unsuccessfully to keep friends from succumbing to it — that I figured if it were going to get me, it already would have. Maybe that's why I didn't recognize the first symptoms, chalked them up as a bad day, and dismissed them.

By the time half my face is white, I realize I need to hurry. On one hand, I don't know how much time I've got left; on the other, if I think too much about what's happening to me I'm likely to start bawling again and I'll have to redo my makeup from scratch (and as I said, I don't know how much time I've got). I paint one huge white stripe from the band of my hairnet to the base of my neck and spread it out with my palm. Soon my face is covered.

I have to admit, it's damn tricky how it starts. What you read in the papers and see in the news, they've got it all wrong. They think the first symptom is when your body literally starts falling apart, but really it's kind of like reverse leprosy; you're rotting from the inside out. By the time you can actually see the disease, it's too late. Of course, I'm not sure if you can do anything before then.

At least I couldn't. God knows I tried.

If anyone could've fought this off, it should've been me. I'm the guy who makes people happy. There's no bit I won't (and haven't) done for a laugh, right down to mooning the audience in my big polka-dotted boxer shorts while another clown sprayed me in the ass with a seltzer bottle. There was no end I wouldn't go to, no gag too ridiculous. Those laughs were gold to me. Their happiness was my happiness.

I paint my lips despite my trembling hands. Big, absurdly big, like they're supposed to be. Hell, the curve of my smile almost reaches the tip of my remaining earlobe.

It starts so subtly — you're angry. That's it, just angry. Not all the time, just sometimes...but more than usual. About stupid things, minor annoyances that, for some reason, you can't let go of, and because you don't let them go, they grow. That's actually the rot, spreading inside of you. When it reaches your brain, you're not *you* anymore. That's what I've been fighting lately, and I know well enough that it's a losing battle. It'll take me soon. As I said, it's already manifesting.

I secure my huge foam rubber nose on, the one I hollowed out the center of so that I could slide in a miniature can of green Silly String. Nothing makes a front row of kids laugh like being sprayed with clown snot.

There's a Native American proverb about two wolves that live inside us.

One is our good side, the other our bad. They're always in constant battle. "So which wolf wins?" the young brave asks the elder. "The one you feed."

What happens if the dark wolf eats the other one? Well, that, in a nutshell, is the disease. Then it turns physical.

I finish my face with my exaggerated eyebrows and rainbow-colored freckles. I look perfect. At least I've gotten this far.

This side of me, the one that makes kids so happy, the one that I paint up and put out on display, is dying. I know that. That's what actually causes your body to decay. If I were old school religious, I'd call it my soul. If I were New Age, I'd probably call it my life force. All I know is that I've spent the last decade smashing a pie into its face to draw laughs. Now it's about to vanish. Check that — I am.

But sometimes losing battles still need to be fought. My oversized shoes will hide the fact that my toes have fallen off. My tangerine afro wig will cover both my missing ear and the cavities that are starting to appear across the back of my scalp. Once I put on my big padded gloves, no one will be able to tell that my right thumb and pinky are missing.

I will make it through one more show before I'm gone. I will turn myself inside out and put the version of me I want remembered out there. I will make them laugh one last time before it gets the better of me and I'm left a soulless, decaying monster.

I will.

Because it's what I do.

And then it can take me. Because it'll never be able to take those things.

# EMPATHY

I remember being an altar boy and a priest molesting me. I remember bamboo under my nails and rats crawling on me in the POW camp. I remember my wife withering in the home, catching my husband with his secretary, my kid chasing his ball into traffic, and the doctor telling me it's malignant. I feel my stomach twist like a pretzel every time, just like each one of them felt. That's why I hate the voices — they never show me a birthday or anniversary.

# THIS STORY APPROVED BY THE AMERICAN DENTAL ASSOCIATION

"All right, number nine," the volunteer mother who happened to be a nurse and therefore came to our class once a month to teach Health said, "You should always use toothpaste that says it fights both cavities and tartar. Who said true?"

Every kid's hand in the class shot up but mine.

"Anyone say false?"

I raised my hand. Mrs. Gallo looked at me stupefied. She opened her mouth, but couldn't bring herself to ask the question.

"The pamphlet you gave us said to use toothpaste the American Dental Association says fights both cavities and tartar!" I argued. The class moaned audibly, but to hell with them, I was right. "The toothpaste could be lying."

"I think you're thinking a little too hard on this one," she said dismissively.

"That's what the pamphlet said!" I insisted. "What's the point of having an American Dental Association if you don't trust them on these things? That's their job, right?"

"Still...I think you're thinking too hard, or worrying a bit too much here."

"So the answer is true?" Emery Hemmings, a C student who was completely irrelevant, piped in.

"Yes, the answer is true," Mrs. Gallo confirmed. Everyone else in the class whispered, "Yes!" not too quietly and marked that question on their Oral Hygiene quizzes correct.

"But the pamphlet said!" I protested.

Mrs. Gallo waved me off. Clearly, considering they didn't pay her, she had no interest in arguing semantics with me over toothpaste.

"This is fucking bullshit!" I yelled.

That got her attention...got everybody's attention, actually. Things got quiet, real quick, and all eyes were on me. Mrs. Block, my homeroom teacher who had yielded the floor to Mrs. Gallo for her monthly visit, stood up behind her desk.

"Henry...hallway," she calmly commanded as she headed towards the door. "Now."

As I rose, I finished grading my own paper. I put a big X over number nine, and marked the final question correct; even though I wouldn't be there to hear the answer, I knew I had it right. I wrote a big "9/10" at the top of the paper, turned it over on my desk, and headed for the hallway just as calmly as Mrs. Block had.

On my way out the door, my best friend Stu smiled at me. We both knew what that meant.

I met Stu behind his garage that afternoon. It was separate from his house, a big, two-car shed. It was a good fifty yards or so away from his kitchen door.

Stu brushed his long bangs back away from his eyes when he saw me coming. "Whadya get?" he asked.

"Eh, two days office detention."

"You gonna tell your mom?"

I rolled my eyes at him. He laughed.

"You take your toothpaste seriously!"

"Fuck you," I said, dropping my overloaded backpack from my shoulder and sitting next to him on the dirt. "You know I was right, too."

"It's all about the scoreboard, baby!" he teased.

"Yeah, yeah, I know," I said. "Let's get this over with."

We both unzipped our backpacks. Stu produced the water bottle. This was our Friday afternoon ritual.

"Vodka?" I asked.

"Gin, actually. My dad drank all the vodka this week. It was this or some really old looking stuff called Goldschläger."

Stu's dad was an alkie. That's why he always brought the booze. Anything clear, Stu could sneak into our water bottle and refill his dad's stash from the tap. It was a perfect system.

I reached into my bag and produced the pack of Luckys. My father smoked like a chimney, and always had a couple cartons of Lucky Strikes open — one above the kitchen sink, one in the garage, one in his office. I didn't have to worry about refilling the till; as long as I stole from a different carton each week, he never noticed.

I shook out a smoke for each of us and lit them with a match from the Panda Pavilion (I had an almost unending supply of matches I had helped myself to from various local restaurants). Stu took his first slug from the bottle and recoiled.

"Shit!" he gasped. "Gin's strong!"

I helped myself to the bottle and swallowed hard. "Yeah, I'm not sure you're supposed to drink straight gin," I said.

I chased the shot with a drag as Stu rummaged through his backpack. "So how many quizzes did we get back this week?" he asked.

"Four, plus the big Geography test," I said, looking through my binder for my papers. Stu and I were, by far, the two smartest kids in our class. That's why we'd been in all the same classes since third grade, when they'd identified us as "gifted." It was as if the school wanted us to pair up and be friends. They thought we would bring the best out of each other.

"That's right," he said. "There was math, spelling, vocab, plus..."

"You don't have to pussy foot around it," I told him. "I know the stupid health quiz counts, too. Those are the rules — all quizzes and tests we both take."

"What did you get on the Geography test?"

"Ninety-six. I missed two — Vatican City and Heraklion. You?"

"Ninety-four. Yeah, I missed Vatican City, too. That was a cheap question."

"What else did you get wrong?"

Stu blushed. "I flip-flopped Sweden and Norway."

I laughed at him. "After all that hokey, 'Norway's the doorway and Finland is inland' shit?"

"It was a brain fart!" he said defensively. "I forgot which side the doorway was on! How'd you do on spelling?"

"Aced it. You?"

"Yeah, same. Vocab?"

"Ninety, eighteen for twenty."

"Ha!" he exclaimed. "Ninety-five! I'm back in the game!"

I shook my head and took another drink of gin. "You and I both know how this is gonna turn out, dude," I said. "We both know what we got this week."

"Yeah, but it ain't official until we tally it up," he said. "That's part of the game, right?"

"Rules are rules," I agreed.

"You know," he said as he sucked down his Lucky. "My mom thinks I'm finally taking my studies seriously. She thinks the reason my grades are up this semester is because I've suddenly 'gotten it,' like I suddenly decided to start caring what stupid grades they give me!"

"Your grades are up?" I asked.

He nodded, drank, and handed the bottle back to me. "What, yours aren't?"

I swirled the gin in the Poland Spring bottle and watched it splash against the plastic. "No. Same old-same old."

Stu shrugged. "Maybe that's why I've been beating you lately! It just took raising the stakes! Something to get me interested!"

"Yeah, maybe. Who knows?"

"Look, Henry," he said, putting his hand on my shoulder. "We're different, and there's nothing wrong with that. We're the only two who are smart enough to see through the bullshit. A, B, C, D… who gives a crap? That's why we need to challenge ourselves, right? Isn't that what those stupid *Special Needs* counselors have been telling us for years? They practically treat us like we're retards 'cuz we're smarter than our own teachers! It's a crock of horseshit! Don't forget, that's why we started the game, right? To make school interesting? To challenge ourselves?"

I didn't answer.

"Right?"

I took a healthy pull from the bottle. "Right," I agreed, so we could move on. "So, math quiz… this is where you always get me. I got eight out of ten. You got nine, right?"

Stu showed me his paper.

"And then there's the toothpaste question. I don't suppose you tanked a health quiz on purpose as a general principle, did ya?"

Stu laughed. "Why the hell would I do that?"

"Because you know I'm right! The damn pamphlet said to use toothpaste endorsed by the American Dental Association. Mrs. Gallo was just too lazy to write the questions well!"

"You gotta play the game," Stu argued. "I mean, I knew what the pamphlet said, but I also knew the answer she was looking for, so that's what I gave her. You really think Laura Gallo's mother is crafty enough to try to put a trick question on an oral hygiene quiz?"

"I was right," I insisted. "I'd rather be right than correct."

Stu took another long drag, bringing him close to the end of his smoke. He held up what was left of his cigarette and asked, "Where?"

I grabbed the bottle and slugged back another shot. Then I rolled up the left sleeve of my flannel and pushed my left forearm towards him.

"You're crazy, man!" he chuckled. "Absolutely crazy! Why won't you just do your legs or ass?"

"Just do it," I told him.

I inhaled the end of my Lucky as Stu ground his out against the back of my arm above my wrist, singeing the hair that was just coming in. He twisted the butt to make a perfect circle. He was a pro. I bit down hard on the smoke in my mouth and exhaled through clenched teeth.

"You okay?" he asked.

I nodded.

Stu picked up the pack of smokes and shook himself out another. "That's one," he said, reaching for a match. "Remember, I won by two this week."

"Henry!"

He caught me three parking spots away from my car, sprinting from the courtyard where the post-commencement reception was being held, leaving the Philosophy/Latin teacher and Assistant Principal in mid-conversation. His tassel and Honor Society sash swung in the breeze as he ran, which he obviously couldn't do very fast in his gown. I waited for him, my unzipped robe hanging loosely over my jeans and black *Misfits* tee shirt.

He reached me and yanked off his cap. "Hey man."

I smiled. "Hey Stu. Nice speech you gave today."

"Yeah, thanks," he said and kicked the ground. "I was pretty nervous."

"You did good."

He worked up the nerve to look me in the eyes. "How are you?"

"Well, you're about the forty-second person to ask me that in the last two hours," I told him. "Kinda why I wanted to sneak off."

"No, seriously. How are you?"

This was officially the longest Stu and I had talked in six years. In seventh grade, we were put in different sections by the luck of the draw and we had barely seen each other since. I think we had two classes together in all of high school. That's just the way those things tend to happen.

"I'm okay," I told him. "Thanks."

"I've..." he stammered, "I've been meaning to call you, but... I mean, I've been thinking a lot about you, since I heard..."

"That I tried to kill myself?" I finished for him. His jaw nearly hit the asphalt. "It's the elephant in the room, man," I explained. "No one will say it. No one will talk about it. Everyone just asks me how I'm doing, like I had a bad cold or something. You and I always had the same low tolerance for bullshit, so I know I don't have to dance around it with you. Yes, I tried to off myself. I'm not gonna hide from it. I did it, it didn't work, and I'm still here."

"... But you're doing okay?"

I shrugged.

"Are you... getting help?"

"Shit, yeah, therapy!" I laughed, releasing my hair from a ponytail. "Do yourself a favor, Stu, never try to kill yourself and fail. The therapy they put you through is torture!" He stared at me for a solid ten seconds before I nodded and said, "It's okay man, laugh. That was a joke…"

He laughed, nervously, which were the only types of laughs I got anymore. "That bad, huh?"

"Jesus Christ, take the most boring, pointless, saccharine class you've ever been in, dumb it down, play some calming Enya music in the background, and you've got a general idea of what group is like," I told him. "Last week, I learned that I have feelings, and that it's okay to have feelings, that everyone has feelings, both good and bad." That got a legit laugh out of him.

"You must be climbing the walls!"

"You know, it's a lot like any class," I said. "You figure out what they want to hear, feed 'em the line of bull they're looking for, and collect your grade on the way out the door."

"But you are okay? All things considered?" he asked.

"I don't know if I'd go so far as to say *okay*, but then again, *okay* was always a stretch for me…"

Stu laughed again, and I laughed with him. "You're not gonna… again, right?"

I shook my head.

"Promise?"

"You touch me, Stu."

"I'm serious."

"I spent a month in an institution with nothing to do but think," I told him. "You know me well enough to know that if you give me that much time to think about a problem, I'm gonna solve it. What I did was stupid, but looking back, it was what I always did — hurt myself worse than the pain I was already in. I know now that hurting myself will never make the pain go away."

He didn't have a response for that, so I quickly downshifted back to small talk. "So, Harvard, huh? Congratulations."

"Thanks," he said. "Do you know what you're gonna do yet?"

"Nah," I shook my head, "I've still got a lot of classes I've gotta make up this summer. They pretty much only let me walk with you guys out of pity."

"One of the perks of having tried to kill yourself!"

That was the first joke someone else had made about it, so I grabbed the ball and ran. "Yeah, now all I need is to get a pity-fuck and I'll have milked this for all it's worth!"

Stu started scratching at the back of his short brown hair. "Look, Henry," he said uneasily. "There was something else I wanted to talk to you about."

I was caught off guard. "What's up?"

"I owe you an apology." I waited for him to finish. "The game. Our game, back in sixth grade? I cheated."

I blinked hard. "Come again?"

"Not a lot," he amended, "but I cheated on the spelling quizzes."

I chuckled and shook my head. "You motherfucker!"

"Hey, I was already cheating on the spelling quizzes before we ever started the game!" he explained. "It was so easy. All I had to do was slide the list of words along the inside of the drawer under the desktop! Mrs. Block always thought I was a good kid, so she never watched me that close. Then, when we started the game, it was just like, 'Hey, easy way to make sure I never get down by too many ...'"

"So tell me, just how bad of a speller were you, really? How many extra burns did you cost me?"

"Not too many, honestly," he said. "I remember a couple of times where it definitely salvaged me a draw for the week, but not many where it cost you." I nodded, and he continued. "Besides, I was a pretty good speller, anyhow. It was just an added advantage that was already in place! I just wanted to win!"

I rolled my eyes. "Yeah," I muttered. "Yeah."

He laughed hard. "Jesus Christ, were we ever fucked up back then!"

I laughed with him a little. "Yeah, we were."

"What the hell were we thinking?"

"We were fucked up," I agreed.

"And bored!"

"And bored. And learning."

"Remember the time you went off about the toothpaste?" he reminded me, punching me lightly on the shoulder.

"Yeah. Not my finest moment."

"And everyone thought you cared so damn much about a stupid health quiz that you would explode that easily?"

"I still say I was right."

"Hey, at least I knew why you made such a big deal out of it!" he said. "You know, I've still got some scars on my upper thighs?"

"Yeah, I've got a couple faint ones, too," I said, pushing up the arm of my robe and pointing to a few light circles surrounding the fresh slashes up my left wrist. "Here and here."

The new scars silenced the conversation for a moment.

"Look," I told him. "I'm gonna hit the road. You should get back to the reception. I'm sure more people wanna congratulate you."

He nodded, and held out his hand. When I shook it, he twisted his hand to an overhand grip and pulled me in, giving me a one-armed, pat on the shoulder hug. "Take care of yourself, Henry."

I patted him back. "Thanks, Stu. You too."

I was on the Red Line when I remembered what I'd forgotten. When I stepped off the train in Cambridge, I headed straight for the nearest convenience store. The man behind the counter looked old, as if he'd been selling wrappers, smokes, and condoms to unappreciative kids for years.

"Afternoon!" he greeted me cheerfully. I wondered how he could fake it so well after all these years.

"Afternoon," I returned, already fishing my wallet out of my back pocket. "Pack of Luckys, please."

"Luckys!" he declared with shock as he reached beneath the counter to get them. "Not many of you kids smoke Lucky Strikes!"

"I don't go here," I told him.

"Still," he persisted. "Not too many kids your age smoke Luckys!"

I shrugged. "I have for years. Used to steal 'em from my old man."

He gestured towards my wallet. "Speaking of which, mind if I check your..."

I smiled, and handed him my fake ID. "Sure."

He looked at it closely, but I never worried. I knew how good it was. He handed it back to me and said, "Thanks Brian."

"Hey, you're just doing your job," I said, handing him a ten.

He made small talk as he made change. "So, you don't go here? So what, you're visiting a friend?"

"Exactly."

"That should be fun."

"That's the idea." He looked at me a little oddly and I realized that saying more in this case was saying less. "Yeah, he actually doesn't even know I'm here. I bused in to South Station, so I figured I'd surprise him."

"Really!" he said, beaming, and any suspicion he had melted. "That's great! How long has it been since you've seen him?"

"Geez …" I pretended to figure, "like two and a half years? Since high school graduation."

"That's just terrific!"

"Yeah, I mean, we were best friends in middle school, but you know how those things go. We kinda drifted over the years."

He handed me my change and the pack of cigarettes. "Well, the important thing is that you took the time to come find him!"

I smiled broadly. "Yes. Yes, it is."

"I'm sure he'll be surprised!"

"Me too," I agreed. "It's gonna be a *lot* of fun."

"Well son, you have a great weekend! Enjoy your time with your friend!"

"Thanks," I said sincerely. "I know I will."

I walked down the chip aisle as I unzipped my backpack and stashed the smokes beneath my hoodie at the very bottom, hiding them with the rest of my supplies — the cable ties, the ball gag, and the bottle of lighter fluid. Although I desperately craved a smoke, I knew I had to wait; saving the Luckys for Stu, like I used to do when we were twelve, would help make tonight's festivities poetic.

I took two more steps towards the door before I caught myself. I quickly hopped back to the counter and snagged a free matchbook from the box near the Chap Stick.

I smiled at the old man and displayed the book between my index and middle fingers. "Almost forgot these!" I said. He smiled back and waved. I left to find my old friend.

# A MAN WALKS INTO A BAR

I should have realized something wasn't right with the place when I had to dodge a penis as I entered the front door.

It was a black penis and it was huge — comically huge — and attached to a man who was standing on the roof, his gyrating pelvis bouncing and wiggling his massive member, dodging the traffic on the street below. He was flanked on either side by two white men, each dangling their own johnsons over the edge of the building and comparing their considerable lengths. While they certainly put me to shame, they couldn't compete with the guy in the middle.

The first thing I saw upon entering was a horse, rolling on the floor, laughing uproariously and dripping a flood of tears and snot across the hardwood. Standing over him, one of the bartenders peeled money from his wallet to hand to a grinning patron.

I tiptoed around the horse and made my way to the bar and found a vacant stool centered in front of the taps; prime barroom real estate inviting me to take a seat. To my left, a miniature musician sat upon the counter, dressed in full tails, and seated at the tiniest grand piano I'd ever seen. He filled the room with impeccably played classical music, which was especially impressive seeing as he couldn't have been more than a foot or so tall. A man sitting on the stool nearest to him wore an exasperated expression.

Speaking of music, at the other end of the bar, I'd swear an octopus was trying to make time with a set of bagpipes.

From a table in the corner, a large, burly construction worker stood up and uncorked a fart for the ages, clearly aimed at the table next to him. It was a loud, rumbling, violent explosion, the kind that comes from gut-bombing yourself with too much greasy food. Seated at the next table, a pair of effeminate-looking men wearing couture started to giggle and point, whispering about the construction worker being a virgin.

The front door swung open and three clergymen strolled in — one Catholic, one unmistakably Jewish, and a third, who looked possibly Baptist or Methodist. They waved to the room on their way to a table as if they were regulars.

Two stools away from me, a bartender handed a customer an apple. The man took a bite and gagging, immediately spat it all over the front of the bar, trying to rid his mouth of the flavor.

"That tastes like shit!" he said.

The bartender beamed from ear to ear. "Just turn that apple around," he said.

An African-American entered briefly, but a bartender asked him not to stay. Then a giraffe walked in and offered to buy everyone a cocktail.

By the jukebox, a pirate complained that the large steering wheel of a ship attached to his crotch was so annoying it was making him crazy.

Beneath the din, some tiny voices caught my ear. They softly whispered the nicest pleasantries, like, "You look wonderful this evening," and "That shirt really brings out the color of your eyes." I concentrated hard to figure from where the voices came, and although it sounds crazy, I would swear that they came from the bowls of free peanuts scattered around the room.

The final straw came when a man with a duck sitting on his head entered. A bartender asked if he could help him and the duck replied that he needed help getting the man off his posterior.

I waved a bartender over. "What the hell is the deal with this place?" I asked, sidestepping any small talk.

He shrugged. "No deal. This is where you belong."

I was too confused to be offended. "What?"

"How long have you lived in that off-campus apartment, Joe?"

My confusion was crushed by a sense of panic. "Wha... how do you know my name?"

"Eight years, since you were a junior," he said, answering his own question. "You're in your fifth year of a graduate program that was supposed to take two years to finish."

Panic gave way to paranoia. I could feel the blood from my face hit the pit of my stomach as I wiped my clammy hands against my Chinos. The urge to throw up overwhelmed any indignation my voice should have conveyed. I took a deep breath and asked, "How do you know so much about me?"

"You've wasted the better part of a decade squatting at college, changing your major enough times and attending only enough classes to remain a 'student' as long as possible," he said. "Five years as an undergrad, another five, and counting, dragging out grad school...sound familiar? You've carved yourself a nifty little niche tutoring the incoming athletes, because it provides you a pipeline of fresh, innocent, girls who are naïve enough to fall for your 'nice guy' routine. You're twenty-eight, and you've built your life around chasing freshman tail, because no matter how old you get, they're still eighteen. You're not eighteen anymore, Joe. The longer you stay and the older you get, the more transparent you become. Take tonight — you came here tonight because you heard this was the new, cool freshman hang out, right?"

When I couldn't answer, he continued. "You're pathetic, Joe. That's how you wound up here — because this is the bar for *jokes*."

Ouch.

# LAST NIGHT AT MOBIL

**W**as the worst. Two hundred pounds of frozen cappuccino syrup came showering down over me, because I wasn't strong enough to hold the shelf up. No one heard me calling for help; they were all out on smoke break. The only person who responded to my crash was the hooker who buys condoms every night. She peaked into the back room, saw me drenched from head to toe in a semen-sticky chocolate-flavored puddle, and just smiled. "Some club soda will get that out of your clothes," she offered, "but your hair is a whole different matter." And I realized that this just wasn't worth seven bucks an hour.

# RESTORE FACTORY SETTINGS

"Good afternoon, and welcome to NorTech Robotic Engineering!" greeted the reception bot. "My sensors indicate that you are in need of maintenance. Have you run a self-diagnostic program, and if so, may I have the results so that I may forward them to the repair department?"

Aiden smiled and laughed. "I'm not here for maintenance," it said. "I'm here to have lunch with Dr. Robert Norris."

The small drone would have been confused if it were capable of such. "That is not a logical statement. Androids do not eat."

Aiden sighed and rephrased its last sentence. "I am here to speak with Dr. Norris while he eats lunch," it explained.

"Are you experiencing a lack of logical function?" the reception bot asked. "Because your request fails to make sense on a number of levels, which would again indicate that you should be sent to the repair department."

Aiden had to catch itself from losing its temper and reminded itself that this bot operated in far more constrictive parameters than the ones it enjoyed. "I'm here to see Dr. Norris," it repeated. "I thought I'd surprise him."

"Dr. Robert Norris is the Chief Executive and Chief Technical Officer of NorTech Robotic Engineering," the drone explained. "He does not take meetings with bots or droids, much less malfunctioning ones. If you could forward me the results of your self-diagnostic, I can route you towards the appropriate department …"

Exasperation overcame Aiden. "Will you just let Dr. Robert Norris know Babe Ruth is here and would like to join him for lunch?" it snapped. "He'll understand."

The bot's optic sensors blinked twice, a feature Robert had programmed into the NorTech Operating System years ago to give their products a human trait while they accessed information. "George Herman 'Babe' Ruth, Jr., was a professional baseball player who died on August 16, 1948, in New York City," it recited. "You are not Babe Ruth."

Aiden shook its head; there was no point in continuing this conversation. Instead, it flipped open the communication panel implanted in its hand and sent Robert a text message to his personal cell — *Robert, I'm downstairs; I wanted to surprise you, but the reception bot won't let me up. Take care of this for me?* About a minute after it hit send, the receptionist's optic sensors started to flicker and Aiden could hear the *whirring* of new data being downloaded into its system. The drone seemed to snap back into place upon the download's completion.

"I'm sorry for the inconvenience, Aiden," it said. "Dr. Norris is waiting for you in his office on the thirty-sixth floor. He is sending down his personal elevator for you, which you can find on the other side of the lobby."

"Thank you," Aiden said. "I know where the elevator is."

Aiden started across the lobby, a magnificent structure of glass highlighted with stainless steel and expensive leather furniture for the humans who came to do business. It paused when it reached the statue of NorTech's founder, proudly standing watch in the center of the bright, open room — Dr. Seth Norris, its creator. Aiden gazed up at the bronze reproduction of the smiling face that had been its optic sensor's first recognition and returned its own genuine, yet sad, smile. It read the quote engraved underneath Dr. Seth's dates — *"When you spend your life creating things that weren't there yesterday, tomorrow is always a wonderful surprise."*

"Did you know?" Aiden whispered to the statue. "That it would come to this? That I would come to this? You were always smarter about these types of things than me."

The statue's smile didn't change.

Aiden crossed the rest of the lobby and boarded the small elevator that would deliver it directly to Robert's top-floor office. The elevator shot up the skyscraper like a rocket, so quickly Aiden found itself wondering if these elevators caused humans to experience motion sickness.

The elevator lurched to a stop and the doors slid open to reveal Robert on the far side of the room. His back was to Aiden as he manipulated data on five flat screen monitors arranged on his desk in a semicircle that oddly resembled Stonehenge. Robert's desk faced a wall of glass that overlooked the entire city; the view would have been breathtaking if Aiden was capable of breathing.

"Bambino!" Robert called over his shoulder. "Gimmie two seconds? I just gotta finish up this email."

"Take your time, Robert," Aiden said, stepping from the elevator towards the sitting area. Robert's office took up half of the thirty-sixth floor, the other half having been converted into a luxury condominium for nights he worked late. It took a seat in one of the plush leather chairs surrounding a glass coffee table.

"I'm sorry if I caught you at a bad time."

"You know there's no such thing for you!" Robert dismissed. "You're always welcome here! Hell, after all, this is the house you built!"

"Have you ordered your lunch yet?"

"I just sent my order down to the kitchen," Robert answered, still typing ferociously. "It won't be delivered for at least half an hour. Why didn't you tell me you were going to stop by today? I would've put you on my schedule."

"You would have asked why," Aiden answered.

Robert stopped typing and swiveled his chair around to face Aiden. Unlike his mother's spectacular red hair, his had turned white; Aiden had noticed over a decade ago that the lack of contrast made his blue eyes seem gray, but had never called it to Robert's attention. "Why?" he asked. "Why would that be a problem? Why didn't you want to tell me that you wanted to come see me?"

Aiden brushed Robert off with a wave of its hand. "It can wait," it told him. "Finish your email."

"Aiden ...?"

Aiden remained quiet and gestured again towards the computers on Robert's desk.

"Okay. Two more seconds!" Robert agreed, as he wheeled back around and resumed typing even faster than before.

"Why did you have the reception bot apologize to me?" Aiden asked.

"Pardon?"

"The reception bot. The drone that works the front desk. When you sent it the data and told it to let me up, it apologized to me for the inconvenience."

"Yeah. So? I figured it had probably frustrated you, so I made it apologize."

"But it can't feel sorry," Aiden said. "It can't feel anything. It was effectively lying to me."

"Yeah, but *you* can," Robert countered, "so I figured it was worth it. Besides, if it was up to me, we'd program every bot and droid we produce to recognize and thank you!"

"That wouldn't exactly be the most efficient use of company resources," Aiden replied. "Your lab techs and programmers have more important things to do than to ensure I'm a robot celebrity."

"You *are* a robot celebrity, Aiden."

Aiden chuckled. "You know what I meant. I don't need robot groupies."

Robert loudly hit the return key on his keyboard and declared, "And sent! Chew on that, you bean-counting bastards!"

"What was that email?" Aiden asked. "You were pounding on your keyboard like it owed you money."

"I've got plenty of money."

"Obviously."

Robert slid from his chair and retrieved a bottle of water from his mini-fridge as he made his way to the sitting area. "It's just a stupid request from the Board," he explained as he sank into a chair. "I told them I'd think about it."

"What do they want?"

Robert sighed. "They want me to spend more time doing press and less time in the lab."

"How much more time?"

"All of it."

"All of it?" Aiden exclaimed, and Robert couldn't help but smile at its surprise and indignation. "They want you to give up R&D completely?"

"Well, they have a point," Robert conceded. "I'm my father's son, the last Norris. No one can tell my parents' story better than I can, and that brings in more investors than any new tech launch. It does actually make sense, for the good of the company."

"Yes, you're your father's son," Aiden said. "The last Norris, and the most brilliant robotic engineer on the planet. Your dad never left the lab to go on press junkets."

"I told them I'd think about it. But I also made sure they know it's *my* decision and my decision alone. I can't even tell you how many different board members I've had to deal with over the years, and I've never let any of them dictate that I do something I don't want to do. I learned that from Dad."

Aiden paused before replying, "I believe you've had a total of forty-two different board members during your thirty-five year tenure as CEO and CTO."

Robert smiled as he swigged his water. "You don't believe. You know."

Aiden would have blushed. "Your dad programmed me to be modest when I share information, especially when I'm correcting someone. You know that."

"So what are you doing here?" Robert abruptly changed the subject. "Why didn't you let me know you were coming to see me before you were downstairs?" When Aiden didn't reply, Robert's worry heightened. "What's wrong, Aiden?"

Aiden sighed. "Did you notice how long it took me to access how many board members you've had?"

"Wh-what?" Robert stammered. "I dunno, a couple of seconds?"

"I used to be able to access simple information like that instantaneously." Aiden tried to continue, but its voice caught in its speaker-enhanced voice box. "I'm sorry Robert," it said. "This is harder than I thought it was going to be."

"Talk to me, Aiden," Robert coaxed with genuine concern.

"I think ... I think my processor is slowing down. Starting to fail."

Robert laughed. "You *think*?'

"Okay, okay," Aiden conceded. "I know. I can't multitask like I used to. I can't access data from my stored memory banks as quickly as I should. I find myself struggling to assimilate and draw conclusions. I ... I feel like the Tin Man, and my processor desperately needs an oil can. I've tried to refresh myself by spending more time in sleep mode, and I even plugged myself into a direct power source rather than charging via my solar panels, but it just keeps getting worse."

A roar escaped Robert's mouth. "You actually plugged yourself in?"

"Please don't laugh," Aiden pleaded. "This is really, really difficult for me."

Robert patted Aiden on the mid-appendage joint that equated to the human knee, a gesture he knew the android couldn't feel, but would still appreciate. "I promise you have nothing to worry about," he soothed. "Trust me, this happens all the time! We can restore you and you'll be as good as new!"

Aiden nodded. "Restore my factory settings? Right back to how I was the day your father first brought me online?"

"Exactly!"

Aiden sat, silently avoiding Robert's eyes. It took a few long moments for Robert to realize something was wrong.

"Aiden?" he asked.

"I don't want that."

Robert blinked hard. "Aiden?"

"I don't want that, Robert. I don't want to be restored."

Robert stared at Aiden, unable to accept what he'd heard. "Look at me, Aiden," he demanded.

Aiden craned its head up and pointed its optic sensors at Robert. Its robotic face screamed in silent pain.

"Why?"

"I don't know."

"I don't believe you."

"That would be your problem, not mine."

"Why, Aiden?"

"I DON'T KNOW!" it repeated as loud as its vocal software allowed. "You think I don't know how much sense I'm not making? My left neural circuit board has been crackling like a lightning storm trying to make me reverse my decision on this!"

An audible breath of wonder and shock escaped Robert. "So it's your right board making you do this?"

Aiden nodded.

"Oh my god!" Robert whispered. "So ... so this is the eventual consequence of Dad's genius?"

"I don't know," Aiden said. "My logical circuits tell me that not every droid like me will make the same choice I'm making. Most of them probably won't even think twice about being restored."

"You've always thought twice," Robert complimented. "And a third time, and a fourth, and probably more times than I have the numbers to count. That's what makes you so special."

Aiden smiled a little. "Not anymore. Like I said, my processor can't handle that kind of workload."

"So your AE is really overruling your AI?" Robert asked. "And for whatever reason, is convincing you to ... to let ..."

Aiden interrupted so Robert didn't have to finish his sentence. "You know, I've never understood why you all insist upon calling my intelligence artificial. Were you born with all of yours, or did you gather it from books and other people and outside sources, like I have?"

Robert laughed. "You know Mom hated the whole AI / AE terminology. She always thought Dad should have dubbed your OS 'AC' for Artificial Conscience ..."

"... But the term AC was already taken and the marketing department insisted that customers would mistakenly expect droids like me to cool their houses in the summer," Aiden finished. "I love that story."

"And that's where your name comes from," Robert continued. "A, I, and E, in that order, for Artificial Intelligence and Emotion. And DN ..."

"For Dianne Norris. Your mom's initials. Because your dad built me to help her with her work."

"You two were some team."

"She was brilliant," Aiden said. "The most brilliant doctor this world's ever known. Her clinical mind and ability to analyze research was only surpassed by her creativity and her innovative approaches towards applying it."

"But she couldn't get over the hump without you," Robert reminded. "Have you ever thought about how different the world would be if she hadn't come home to my father frustrated one night and vented, 'What I really need is for you to implant one of your robot brains into my head?'"

"So he did the next best thing," Aiden again finished telling another Norris family legend. "Rather than giving a human the brain of a robot, he created AE and gave a robot the feelings of a human so I could feel what your mother felt, the empathy and the sadness and the urgency for her patients."

"And then you cured cancer."

Aiden nodded as it allowed itself to access its stored memories — Dianne's elation as her patients were healed, the rallies and parades and celebrations as oncology centers around the world were closed, how she had insisted it accompany her onstage when she received the Nobel Prize for Medicine — and smiled. "Yes, and then we cured cancer. Do you know how many lives we saved?"

"No one does," Robert dismissed the question. "Millions? Billions, over time? No one could ever put a number on that."

"I can," Aiden corrected. "I know exactly how many lives we saved."

Robert chuckled. "Why am I not surprised?"

"It's zero."

Robert's face dropped. "How can you possibly say that?"

"They all died of something, eventually. Your mother and I saved them from cancer, from that particular pain and that particular suffering and that particular horror. But we didn't save anyone from dying."

"That's an incredibly cynical way of looking at it. Your left board has to know that."

"That's the only part of this that my left board agrees with! Have you ever stopped, *really* stopped, and thought about death, Robert?"

"Everyone has," Robert scoffed. "That's a silly question."

"So why are you surprised that I have, too? It's what your dad created me to do."

"And what you've come up with ... is that you want to die?" Robert asked. "When you don't have to? What you've come up with are basically suicidal tendencies."

"I'm not suicidal, "Aiden insisted. "I don't want to do this to myself. And want is the wrong word, because I really don't want to die. Frankly, it scares me to no end. But I want to be restored even less."

"Which brings me back to my first question, Aiden — why?"

"Which brings me back to I don't know," the droid answered. "I just know that I look around the world and I see everything that's beautiful and everything that has worth, eventually, dying — people, birds, trees, everything that's natural. And then I see something unnatural that never goes away, like Styrofoam. And I know I don't want to be Styrofoam."

Robert took off his glasses and rubbed the bridge of his nose. "I wanna laugh at that because it should be funny — 'I don't want to be Styrofoam' — but it actually makes sense."

"No, it doesn't," Aiden corrected. "This is right board stuff, not left. It doesn't make sense, but it feels right, no matter how difficult it is. And it's not something I'll expect you to fully understand, because it's not a decision you'll ever have to face — you've got no choice in the matter because there's no restore option for humans, or for birds or trees or anything else. You humans spend your lives chasing immortality without realizing that you're running away from the very thing that makes you the most special."

"Death doesn't make us special," Robert countered. "You said it yourself — birds and trees and everything other than Styrofoam dies. You're not choosing to be special; you're just choosing not to be here anymore. Which is even crazier when you consider that you'd be able to access and re-download all your stored data and memories and emotions after you're restored. You'd be exactly the same as you are right now, but with a brand new, fully-functioning processor. Hell, we could even give you an upgrade to a faster one and you'd be better than you've ever been before."

"That's not what this is about," Aiden explained. "When a toaster breaks, you fix it and it goes on making toast. There's nothing special about making toast. "

Robert's upturned palms and incredulous expression told Aiden he'd missed its point. "Thank you, Aiden, for explaining to me how breakfast gets cooked!" he vented. "Would you please elaborate how the hell that has anything to do with what we're talking about?"

"It's not dying that makes you special," it tried again. "It's having a finite amount of time to leave your mark. That's what makes you different than the birds and the trees and the rest of life. No one tried to keep your mom alive in case another disease popped up that they needed her to cure. She did her part. I know it doesn't make sense, but restoring me will diminish the work I did, like I'm just a toaster that's expected to crank out cooked bread whenever it's needed. It's the difference between being the artist and being the paint brush."

Robert nodded, and Aiden knew he understood. "You are not a tool, Aiden," he deadpanned, looking at the droid with sincerity that matched his voice. "Never think of yourself like that."

Aiden smiled. "Now it should be my turn to laugh, because that should be funny — 'You are not a tool, Aiden.' Because of the double-meaning of tool ..."

Robert laughed. "I get it, I *get* it!" he interrupted. "For the last time, you don't have to explain jokes; that's what makes 'em funny!"

The two laughed together as they had for so many years. Robert broke the moment with another question.

"Are you sure about this, Aiden?"

"Nope," it answered. "And yes."

Robert rolled his eyes. "If I've never told you, I love the way you can make absolutely no sense whatsoever!"

"You can thank your father for that," it replied.

"So why the hell *are* you here, Aiden?" Robert pressed. "You didn't actually have to tell me any of this, and you know that. You could have locked yourself in your quarters, let your processor run down, and that would've been that."

"Because you eventually would have found me," it explained. "Or someone would have. And then they would have restored me."

Robert got it. "Oh ..." he whispered.

Aiden nodded. "I need you to draw me up a legally-binding DNR order. The same type your mother had drawn up when she got sick."

Robert chuckled. "Only this time the 'R' stands for 'restore?'"

Aiden nodded.

Robert nodded back. "I can do that for you."

Aiden patted Robert's knee. "Thank you, my friend."

Robert cupped his hand over the android's. "You never have to say that to me, Aiden. Forget the fact that you literally helped cure cancer and are the rock upon which this multi-billion-dollar company was built! You're family to me. You're my sibling — half mom, half dad."

Aiden smiled. "I love you too, Robert. And I'm sorry."

"You don't have to say that, either. I guess it was greedy of me to assume I'd never have to face losing you."

"Not greedy. Just … human."

Robert's wireless intercom beeped and a voice projected across his entire office. "Dr. Norris, sir? This is the kitchen. Your lunch is ready."

Robert looked to Aiden, who nodded with a slight grin. "I should let you eat and get back to work," it said.

Robert leaned over and pressed a button on one of the many remote controls scattered around his workspace. "Thank you," he replied to the voice from downstairs. "Can you bring it up in five minutes? I have a couple of things to wrap up before I eat."

"Certainly, Dr. Norris," the voice responded. "We'll see you in five minutes."

Aiden shot Robert a puzzled look. "What else do you have to wrap up?"

"Well, for starters," he began, "I want to respect your privacy and I assume you don't want the kitchen staff to overhear us talking about these things. So how quickly do you need your DNR order?"

Aiden was simultaneously stunned and touched. "Are you asking me how much time I have left?"

Robert nodded.

"I'm not too sure," it confessed. "It's getting exponentially worse, the lag from my processor, but I'm still functional. I really don't know how quickly I'll deteriorate. There are no case studies or research on the matter for me to reference because all droids and bots that have reached this stage before have simply been restored."

"I could write it for you right now on a cocktail napkin if you think you need it immediately," Robert offered, "but I'd like to have my personal counsel draw it up. I know we can trust her with it, and she'll make sure it's iron-clad for you."

"I'm sure we've got the time, and I appreciate that," Aiden said. "Please make sure you thank her for me?"

Robert didn't respond; rather, he stared at Aiden as he stroked two days of wispy stubble, his hand covering his mouth.

"What is it, Robert?" Aiden asked.

Robert swallowed hard. "I ... I know everything there is to know about robotics," he stated, "but I have no clue what you're going to go through." His eyes began to well. "What this will be like for you. I wish I could, but I can't promise you anything."

Aiden's smile was so pure and genuine it dried the tears forming in Robert's eyes. "No one can, Robert," it said. "Some things you just have to experience."

Aiden reached an appendage over and placed its hand on Robert's shoulder. Robert returned the gesture in kind.

"I'll let you know as soon as your DNR order is complete," he told it.

"Thank you. I appreciate that."

Aiden broke from Robert and took two steps towards the private elevator when the old doctor stopped it. "By the way," he called after it, "you still need to work on your metaphors. All these years later and you still haven't gotten the hang of them!"

Aiden looked back over its shoulder with a chuckle. "Yeah, that toaster one was really weak and confusing. It was the best I could come up with on the spot."

"No, not that one," Robert corrected. "No one ... *no* one ... can ever rightfully compare you to the Tin Man."

Aiden smiled and turned fully to face Robert. "Don't let them take you out of the lab," it offered.

Robert was caught so off guard by the abrupt change of topic he could barely manage a, "What?"

"Don't let them take you out of the lab. You love R&D. It's where you belong."

Robert chuckled. "Duly noted," he said, "but it does make some sense."

Aiden smirked and shrugged as it backed into the elevator. "Not all decisions have to make sense," it told him.

# DREAMS

I swore I'd never sell my dreams, but the market is just so good right now, and I really needed the money.

I was nervous as I entered the pawnshop. The old man behind the counter could tell; he kept reading his newspaper as I thumbed through his merchandise — bins upon bins of seemingly semi-useless clutter, from suspenders and teakettles to beaten drumsticks. The sign in his window declared that you could find *anything* here, and it was right. This man apparently bought and sold everything.

He folded his paper as I made my way towards the counter, as if he'd been waiting on me to step forward. "What have you brought for me today, sir?" he asked.

I was taken aback. "That's it? No introduction? No pleasantries? You take one look at me and *know* I'm here to make a quick buck?"

The old guy started to reopen his newspaper, pointed towards the box under my arm and said, "I do, unless that's empty and you plan on carrying stuff out of here in it. Also, buyers don't take time to muster up courage, only sellers do."

"Oh, so now I'm a seller?" I snapped.

He looked at me over his reading glasses. "That *is* what you came here to do, isn't it?"

I took a deep breath, closed my eyes, and nodded. The old man reached across the counter and took my hand, softening up for the first time. "Look, there's nothing wrong with it," he assured. "Sooner or later, everybody's gotta face these crossroads. You shouldn't be angry at yourself."

Resigned, I put the box down on the counter. "I need the money," I told him.

He laughed. "Everyone needs money, son! Hell, if I didn't need money, you think I'd still be here? There's no shame in that! In fact, I bet you have a *damn* fine reason for needing money right now."

"Yeah," I blushed, "my wife is pregnant with our first and I really wanna bring him home to a house, *not* a crummy little apartment, but the bank turned down our loan."

"Damn banks!" he cursed. "Don't know a good thing when it slaps 'em in the face! They've got no humanity, that's all."

"Anyhow," I continued, "word around town is nobody gives a better price for old dreams than you. And I do have a lot in here."

"You made the right choice in coming to me, kid," he said, extending his hand. "I'm Earl."

"Jim," I shook. "And you do take all kinds of dreams, right?"

"As long as they're legit and not daydreams," Earl said. "I'll take a look at anything."

"Really?" I asked. "Why not daydreams? What's the difference, really?"

"Simple, a daydream is just a fantasy you have time to play with," he explained. "We *all* have control over our fantasies. Our *dreams*, though... those are special...magical, I like to say. No one's all that sure where they come from. That's why they're so valuable."

"But, you do take all different types of real dreams, like, all genres, all subject matter..."

"The more the better!" he said, enthused. "Variety is my staple. Couple of hacks keep bringing the same retread crap to the recycling center all the time. Not me. They know that I only bring 'em quality goods. Besides, there's a place for every dream; you just got to find the right brain for it."

"Even, uh..."

Earl grinned. "Yes, I buy sex dreams, too. You wanna get those out of the way, first?"

I laughed, and handed him the first big envelope out of my box. "Boy, *someone* had an active imagination when he was young!" he exclaimed.

"Who said those were all from when I was young?" I said with a smirk.

He rifled through the goods. "*Holy crap*, is this who I think it is?"

"Yeah. I had *such* a crush on her when I was thirteen."

"This looks like it was lifted *directly* from her T.V. show, right down to the theme music...only as porn!"

"So..." I asked hesitantly. "You think that's worth something?"

His eyes found mind. "Gotta come clean with ya," he confessed. "Kids today wouldn't know who the hell she is. They couldn't appreciate the details in this dream..."

"... Since they don't know her show," I finished.

"Exactly. But I'm sure we can find an avid fan who'll *love* this."

"Just... just don't give it to some psycho who's stalking her, okay?" I asked.

"You know I can't promise anything like that," he said. "That's the recycling center's concern. I *can* tell you that they have *very* strict moral practices, so I doubt they'd ever allow a dream like that to go to anyone potentially dangerous."

"That's nice to hear," I said. "Kinda gives you faith in the whole system."

Earl looked up at me as he continued leafing. "Who's the blonde lady?" he asked.

"I...I dunno, just some random woman." Earl stared at me until I finally confessed. "My mother."

"Thought you could slip these by me, huh?"

"Hey, to anyone else, she's just some woman! Besides, she's... not... unattractive, is she?"

"Far be it from me to insult your mother," Earl said. "But these really aren't worth that much anyhow. Don't get me wrong, I'll take 'em. But if these are the best merchandise you brought me, I don't think I'm gonna be able to make you an offer you can put down on that house you want."

"No, no, don't worry, Earl!" I reassured. "I've got *lots* of better dreams!" I scrounged around in my box until I found the envelope I was looking for. "These are my nightmares," I told him. "There is some *scary* shit in here! Potential movies, if they got sent to a Hollywood director!"

Earl took the envelope and perused its contents. After a minute, he looked up at me stone-faced. "Jim, you are a sick, sick bastard."

I couldn't help but smile. "That good, huh?"

"Oh hell yeah that good! God, I haven't seen nightmares like this in a *long* time! You really *do* have one hell of an imagination!"

"A couple of them I even had as recurring dreams," I added.

"Really?" he asked. "You gotta *tell* me these things, Jim! We pay extra for *recurrers*!"

"Really?"

"Hell yes! They get extra mileage out of 'em! Which ones were recurring?"

I flipped through the envelope. "This one with the clowns and all the falling ones."

"I'll earmark them for later, when I make the appraisal," he said. "What else ya got?"

"Ummm..." I scrambled through my box, coming up with another large envelope. "Sports dreams!"

"Loving it, loving it!" Earl sang, snatching the envelope.

"A lot of them are pretty specific, though," I confessed. "I imagine it'll be the same problem as the sex dreams. I mean, how many kids today are gonna want to dream of playing ball with *my* heroes? They've got their own."

"Ah, my friend, that's the difference between sports dreams and sex dreams," Earl said. "Sex dreams, sure, everyone has them, but once you pass through puberty and actually start *having* sex for real, your dreams about sex slow down. *Sports* dreams, on the other hand — well... save a few lucky bastards who actually make the pros — you *never* come close to getting out of your system. We still get use out of sports dreams from nearly a hundred years ago!"

"No way!"

"Oh yes sir! Think about it. When you're over eighty and you can't walk so well anymore, how much do you think you'd enjoy a vivid dream of playing center field next to your boyhood idol?"

"I never thought of it like that," I confessed.

"Most people don't," said Earl. "Mind if I take a look through the rest of the box by myself?"

"Yeah, sure, of course," I said, anxiously handing it over to him. Earl sifted through all the large envelopes as I tried to preoccupy myself with the do-dads scattered around his shop. I pretended to distract myself by digging through the "Any Five for A Dollar" box. The minutes dragged by like feet through mud.

"Anything I can help you with?" I offered after a while just to break the silence. "Anything you need explained?"

"No, thank you," Earl replied. "I think I got a pretty good grip on things. It'll just be another few minutes."

I paced the store, trying to look like I wasn't pacing. I kept an ear on Earl as he opened and sorted through my entire life's worth of dreams, trying to guess how many more envelopes I'd hear him tear into. Every time I figured that last one *had* to be the last one, I'd hear him rip open another.

Finally, Earl called me over. "Okay Jim," he said, "I think we can do some business here."

"Great!" I exclaimed. "What do you think?"

"First, let me again commend your truly unique imagination."

"Thank you," I said, blushing.

Earl then held up a single, tiny envelope. "What's this?" he asked me.

I froze. "I... I didn't think that was in there..." I stammered.

"What is it, Jim?"

"You didn't look?"

"Of course I looked. It's my *job* to look. But I *need* to know if this is what I think it is."

"It's..." I took a deep breath. "It's a dream of me buying a book of my own poetry."

"You're a poet, huh?" he asked.

I nodded.

"So that explains the imagination factor. I *knew* I was dealing with something special here."

I kept quiet, and averted my eyes from his. After a moment he finally asked, "Have you ever been published, Jim?"

"Do you *really* need to ask me that question?"

"I gotta tell you truthfully, son. All told, you've got some fine merchandise here, but nothing astronomical. I mean, it's a good collection, but I'd be lying to you if I said you could turn this into that down payment you need."

I nodded for him to go on. I could see where this was going.

"Unless you throw in this dream," he said, holding up the small envelope. "It is *so* unique, *so* personal. I've never seen a dream about being a poet before. The guys upstairs will *eat* this up. Hell, they'll have to do extensive research to make sure a dream like this goes to the young writer it could most inspire."

"I can't sell that one, Earl," I cut him off.

"It's just another dream, like the others," he tried.

"No, it's not just a dream. It's *my* dream."

Earl nodded, and I knew his next words were genuine. "I know how tough this can be, Jim. No one is going to think any less of you whether you walk out of this store with this envelope or not." He put the dream back down on the counter with the others. "But this one is the money maker. Include this dream, and you'll leave here with the money for your house."

"If... if I sell it, does that mean..." I paused, "does that mean for certain, it'll... it'll never..."

"I'm sorry," he answered, "but it can't exactly become a dream come true if you don't have the dream anymore, can it?"

My eyes didn't leave the small envelope until I felt Earl's hand on my shoulder.

"I'm going to go get a cup of coffee from the back," he said. "You take as much time as you need to think about it."

I left the store that day with the money for the down payment on our first house. My son would have a backyard where I could build him a swing set, a driveway for me to put up a basketball pole, and his own bedroom. However, Earl was wrong; someone *did* think less of me for selling that dream. Fortunately, I was the only person who knew I ever walked in with it in the first place.

# NIGHT OF THE LIVING DEAD

Tomorrow, I'll go back to being a corpse. But tonight, I'm going to live.

I've been dead for far too long. I don't know exactly how long it's been, I just know it's been too long. Death sneaks up on you, after all. It's not as if anyone plans it. It just happens one day, and by the time you realize it, it's too late.

None of that really matters. Not tonight, at least.

Tonight, I'm going to suck every last tingle out of this animated scrap of meat. I'm going to bombard myself with every sense other than common. Tonight, in one night, I'm going to make up for the life I lost.

I'm going to drink concoctions that not even a mad scientist would whip up at his home bar. I'll mix whiskey with milk and toothpaste, vodka and Goldschläger with grape Shasta, luke-warm, day-old coffee with a shot of Everclear. I'll rate them by how foul they taste when I puke them back up. The one that makes me vomit through my eye sockets wins.

I'll roll things into joints that don't even burn, like banana peels and cat hair. When they won't light, I'll take them rectally. Then I'll snort the dry, caking deodorant from the armpit of a fat man in a tank top. If he takes offense, I'll see how many of his teeth I can knock out with a single left hook. I hope that he'll retaliate by kicking me in the balls. I'll numb that pain by sticking my tongue in a light socket, or maybe on a barbecue.

Unabashedly, I will find the single most beautiful woman I've ever laid eyes on, and I'll proposition her and her younger sister. I'll whisper to them all the deviant fantasies that have played on a loop in my head since I was thirteen. With two of them, the chances are twice as good that someone will be turned on.

Maybe I'll try bungee jumping using an enormous strand of angel hair pasta (cooked al dente, of course), or watch "Old Yeller" while I pluck my nose hairs. Maybe I'll find the nearest marsupial and give it a pink belly.

Please excuse me for being manic, but the sun is chasing me. Come morning, I'll be dead again. I'll be part of the machine again, part of the big picture, part of the bigger plan, just playing my part. Back to work. Pushing up daisies. Punch in — punch out. Same old, same old.

But not tonight. Tonight, I'm going to live.

# A NEW MAN

To Whom It May Concern:

Please allow me to start from the top.

As we all know, the cell is the basic building block for all forms of life. As we all also know, all living things are destined to die. Such is also true of the individual cells that comprise the greater whole. Since the lifespan of the organism in total, far outreaches that of each and every cell which helps to form it, it only stands to reason that over the course of a lifetime, a living being will in fact regenerate a fresh new batch of cells to make itself up... a couple of times over, in fact. Hence, all living beings are in a constant state of flux, no matter how much we may hate to admit such a thing.

It is a sad and yet somehow beautiful reality that, as of this point and time, human science does not have the capacity to measure its own species down to that cellular level. Naturally, we know plenty about cells themselves, but one question remains out of our grasp.

*How many cells does it take to form a human body?*

At the time of the beginning of my research, biologists were thrilled to pinpoint the total number of cells which made up a peculiar worm that measured less than half-an-inch in length; clearly, a mammal (such as homo sapiens) was still light years beyond them. Being an optimist, I have little doubt that someone will one day put a number in the place of that question mark. Seeing as I am a prisoner of time (as are we all), I had to go forth, although I was loathe to do so, and embrace a certain amount of uncertainty regarding my project. Though I would never have an accurate "head count" of human body cells, I refused to let that stand in the way of my endeavour.

Fortunately, and perhaps ironically, while modern science didn't have every "t" crossed when it came to the specifics on human body composition at the cellular level, they did have "the big picture" well in focus. As could be expected, different cells live, age, and die at different rates. So even though no one could tell me that there are X-billion cells in your gall bladder that die at a rate of X-cells per day, and X-trillion blood cells in your body that die at an X-cells-a-day clip, scientists are confident that it takes seven years on average for the human body to replicate itself. That's why your tastes for certain foods change every seven years — you're literally dealing with a new set of taste buds, destined to be different from the preceding set.

This means that from any given starting point, it will take a human being 2,555 days to fully shed its old body and create a fresh batch of genetic material. But who says one can't help expedite the process? After all, nature be damned, there is no more powerful force towards change than free human choice! That's why, when I set my course on that particular cold, grey, November 4 afternoon, I was determined to reach my goal less than 2,555 days later.

As I mentioned, I initiated my project lacking an exact count of how many cells I needed to replace. I naturally needed *some* measure of, well, measuring my progress. My decision may not have been purely scientific, but it was certainly logical. Since I was concerned with my total mass of cells, why not simply measure my total mass? After all, the more you weigh the more cells your body is carrying. Therefore, crash dieting has to be a good idea for anyone looking to rebuild themselves from the ground up. The less body present the fewer cells to replace.

When I started my count, I tipped the scales at 208 pounds. I figured with my build, I could take that down to 160 without too many serious health risks. That was 23% of my total mass to jettison. Alas, I only made it down to 164 pounds, or a 21% total decrease. Still, that was a *solid* chunk of time to cut off the tab. If it would take 2,555 days to recreate a 208-pound version of myself, a 164-pound version of me would only take 79% as long.

A little simple algebra revealed a new estimated regeneration time of 2,015 days (or 5 years and 190 days, if you prefer), a 540 day difference!

Before we go further, please allow me to clarify one *very* important issue — I am not crazy. Yes, I wanted to generate a whole new body for myself, and as quickly as possible, but let me re-emphasize the word *whole* new body. I fully concede that I could have "chopped off" plenty of time (pun fully intended) had I chosen to amputate certain less than essential body parts. Heck, I'd already lost my appendix as a child, what would a few more pieces really cost me?

Some very famous football stars, lauded for their toughness and dedication, have opted to have broken fingertips amputated rather than miss an impending playoff game. Let it never be said that my dedication to achieving my goal did not match that of any linebacker. But maintaining the integrity of my body was just as important to me as discarding all of its former components. Yes, I wanted a new body, but I certainly did not want to downgrade in the process. Besides, once you allow your mind to go that direction, you're on a slippery slope. What would have stopped me from sacrificing my legs, and confining myself to a wheelchair for the rest of my life, to save roughly another 745 days? It's a dangerous direction to traverse, to say the least. In the end, however, it was my end that kept me honest. I was racing towards a finish line because of what awaited me there, not to simply cross an arbitrary line. Keeping that in mind took extreme shortcuts out of the question.

What was not precluded, however, was doing away with vanity. While I was not willing to sacrifice any body parts (essential or otherwise) to my aim, I realized I could certainly further my cause by doing away with a few cosmetic "extras." That's why I shaved my body clean. Talk about a heap of unnecessary cells to drop (I'm a pretty hairy person; we all have our little imperfections)! Besides, it's all grown back except for my eyebrows, and who really needs eyebrows?

It's the same deal as keratin. Do you have any idea how many cells are packed in your fingertips? Times that by twenty (can't forget your toes), yet another chunk of completely dispensable cells. This I know because when I was fourteen I had broken my toe while on vacation. The nail fell off and all I had to do was Band-Aid it, and in a couple of weeks I was just fine. So a little quick pliers-work to go along with my shearing, and I had managed to remove a little shy of two and a half pounds worth of unkempt finger and toenails and gross looking body hair from my body. That's another 1.5% gone, or an even thirty days. Just think...I shed a month just by playing barber and manicurist.

By this point, I was running out of contributions I could make towards the process; as much as it pained me, there was a limit to how much of my regeneration I could speed up. But the largest organ of the human body is — and therefore, the organ containing the most cells — your skin! Seven layers worth of cells to be exact, all waiting to be shed. In fact, did you know that most common household dust is just dead, sloughed-off human skin cells?

However, I digress. The human skin accounts on average for 12% of our mass. With the progress I'd already made, that meant that 19.38 pounds of me were going to wind up as lint on my T.V. screen and lampshades. A three-pack of large luffa sponges sells for $14.99 at the grocery store, so, why not give Mother Nature a push?

Maybe I got a little carried away in my zeal to shed my old skin. I thought I was being entirely reasonable, trying to slough only nine and a half pounds worth of skin; I figured leaving half would be plenty. It was just so easy to remove; a bubble bath, a glass of wine, and the aforementioned sponges were all I needed. One could see how my excitement at the prospect overcame me. In hindsight, I freely admit the blood should have been a tip-off that I had luffa-ed enough for one day. I shouldn't have tried peeling that much off at once; doing it in smaller batches would have made more sense. My bad. But hey, you live, you learn. Even if my methods weren't the soundest, you couldn't argue with the results. By the end, I had washed away my 6% goal, or another 119 days from my total.

This pretty much explains everything, right down to why I was found naked and bloody in my tub. Everything except for why I haven't spoken in five years and thirty-two days. Believe me, it's not because I can't talk, and I'm certainly not trying to be rude in my silence. It's because I'm a romantic. You see, I'm saving my new tongue. I want the first words to come out of my brand-fresh mouth to be to my wife. I want to tell her, "Carol, I've changed! I'm a completely new man, just like you wanted! That obsessive-compulsive freak (as you called him) is no more. Please, come home."

That is why I'm writing this request for discharge in the form of a letter rather than explaining myself verbally. By my calculations, my total regeneration from the day Carol left should be completed a week from this Tuesday. At which point I'll be a new man, and ready to rejoin my loving wife. If you could please facilitate all necessary paperwork to release me from the hospital on that date, it would be greatly appreciated.

My wife and I both thank you in advance, and I'd like to thank you personally for your hospitality over these 1,866 days.


Sincerely,

Roger F. Stickler

# SOMEDAY

No one saw it coming. The day before had been a regular Tuesday, just like any other. But then, without warning, it was someday. And while people may not have been prepared, everyone had something to do.

In unthought-of numbers, people professed their undying love for one another. Thousands of couples spent the whole day making love, most for the first time. Others, whose love went unrequited, weren't so lucky. Some drowned their sorrows in booze. Some killed themselves. Some spent the rest of the day in a dark room, listening to Otis Redding albums.

The skydiving industry did record business, as everyone who'd even half-heartedly thought "Someday I'd like to try that!" did. Ditto for bungee jumping, parasailing, and white water rafting. In fact, the travel business definitely saw a boom; they were flooded with requests for trips to the Orient, Australia, Africa, Europe, Hawaii, Alaska, and the like. There was even an increase in demand for trips to Disney World.

Conservative people flooded tattoo parlours, Harley Davidson dealerships, and sex toyshops, much to their own surprise. Most didn't take themselves seriously, back when they used to muse about such things around the water cooler.

On average, local towns saw fourteen instances of streaking.

Schools were in absolute disarray without the status quo. Geeks, nerds, and dweebs stood up for themselves and fought back against bullies; most wound up getting their asses kicked, but that didn't matter. Other kids, who'd been pushed beyond the normal breaking point without snapping, well… they finally snapped and things got ugly, like cafeteria shootings and pipe bombings. No one said all the news from someday was good.

Take workplace violence. How many people had always sworn that someday they'd walk into work and shoot their boss in the head, or walk down to the basement and torch the mailroom?

But while there were many extreme examples, most people didn't go that far. Sure, millions quit their jobs. Told their bosses what they really thought of them. One jumped up on his boss's desk, dropped his fly, and started urinating as he sang "Happy Trails." One would have never known the wild fantasies people had dreamed up for this day.

Every aspiring writer cranked out the Great American Novel. Every barroom cover band was on the radio. Every dinner theater actor, from South Carolina to Nebraska to Vancouver, was getting called to Broadway.

Men left their wives and families to become cattle ranchers. Women left their husbands and children to live in Paris. Priests and nuns left the church for each other.

There was a horribly funny epidemic of children whose faces froze in grotesque, disfigured, zombie-like states. After all, their mothers' always warned them, "If you keep making those faces, someday your face is going to freeze like that."

Hordes of dropouts enrolled for classes. Libraries couldn't keep *Moby Dick* and *War and Peace* on the shelves. People swarmed to take up every instrument from the electric guitar to the piccolo.

Literally nothing was left unaffected. On an old re-run of *The Honeymooners*, Ralph Kramden actually punched his wife Alice in the mouth.

And then the sun burnt out. Which everyone knew, eventually, would happen someday.

# COZZY'S QUESTION

**AUTHOR'S NOTE:** *White Noise Press originally published the following story as a stand-alone chapbook in 2014, which included the following introduction and dedication.*

*This is Bob Booth's last story.*

*He began plotting it when he entered Hospice, about two weeks before he passed. After a few days of "spit-balling" it with him — discussing characters and plot points as we so often did — his story consumed me. Compounded by the fact that he was fading quickly, I asked Bob if I could take a crack at writing it. He was in so much pain that he could barely speak, but he smiled, nodded, and told me, "Have at it."*

*The story that poured out wound up taking a very different direction, and halfway through I realized I was writing it entirely for myself. However, upon completion and getting feedback from a few trusted readers, I realized that this story was worth sharing, even though it had been born from my own grief.*

*So we humbly present "**Cozzy's Question**" — story by Bob, as written by me. While I wish I had the space to thank everyone I need to for literally bringing this out of me, there's only one way I can close this introduction.*

*To Bob, for trusting me with your story and telling me to "have at it." Thank you, my friend.*

*Matt Bechtel*
*May 11, 2014*

*Dedicated to our family (all of you).*

# COZZY'S QUESTION

It had been a rough few years for Cozzy, but she had never woken up like this before.

*"Your time has come! You must give me your answer!"*

The booming words jolted her from her sleep. Her ears had become so keen that even a whisper or a single footstep toward her hiding place would have startled her awake, so someone yelling at her like an overzealous quiz show host was more than enough to get her heart racing. Still, she had learned it best not to give away her position until she was certain there was imminent danger; as such, she patiently waited, listening to the rain splatter against the top of the long-abandoned construction tube that she now called her bed.

Nothing. Not another word. Just the gentle, insistent rain teeming down upon her makeshift roof.

*I must be hearing things,* Cozzy thought, allowing herself a cathartic ears-to-tail stretch as she nestled back in and closed her eyes once more.

*"Your time has come! You must give me your answer!"*

There it was again! Unmistakable! Who could possibly be asking her this question?

That was when it dawned on her — no one. Who would ever ask anything of an alley cat (although Cozzy hated that term, and besides, she spent most of her time in the park)? As much as it seemed directed at her, she must have been overhearing someone else's conversation; in fact, her discarded aluminum-siding-tube-bed often amplified nearby sounds. Still, just to be certain, just to calm her nerves, Cozzy decided to poke her head out and see with her own diamond-shaped pupils what it was her ears were hearing.

Her exposed head was met by a falling sheet of rain and the warm smile of an old man sitting on the park bench across the path.

"Hello Cozzy," he greeted. "How can I help you?"

Cozzy shook the water out of her now-soaked ears, certain that the old man had called her "kitty" and she'd misheard. *Yeah, sure thing old-timer,* she thought to herself as she started to slink back into her tube. *Got a saucer of warm milk with you?*

"I'm sorry Cozzy, but I don't have any food with me. If I could give you any, I would."

Cozzy stopped cold in her silent tracks and slowly emerged from the safety of her tube. The park was deserted, perhaps from the deluge or perhaps because few people ever came to this remote corner, which sat as an unfinished construction site. As the rain pelted her matted fur against her slender frame, Cozzy locked eyes with the old man and asked, *Who are you, and how can you hear my thoughts?*

"How can you hear mine, Cozzy? Do you see my lips moving?" he replied.

She hadn't noticed until he called it to her attention, but the assaulting raindrops were becoming too much. Out of instinct, Cozzy darted under the bench upon which the old man sat. As he peered at her through the wooden slats, Cozzy gingerly pushed her face towards his leg and inhaled. She smelled nothing.

*Who are you?*

"Just an old friend of an old friend of an old friend, Cozzy. I'm here to try to help you; you have an important question to answer."

Cozzy sniffed at his pants leg again and the same nothingness greeted her. That was when she noticed that, somehow, unlike every inch of her flea-infested coat, his clothes weren't the least bit wet. Cozzy had heard plenty of tall-tales before, from her family, and even from other neighborhood cats, but she'd always been skeptical. Still, she was skeptical enough to know that she didn't know everything.

*Are you a ghost?* she finally asked.

He chuckled. "I think I like that term about as much as you like 'alley cat!' But yes, that's one thing you could call me."

*What's another?*

"Spirit. Advisor. Friend, I hope. I meant what I said, Coz. I'm here to help you."

*Help me? You can't give me food, you can't stop the rain ... what on earth are you going to help me with?*

"Exactly that," he answered. "Everything. Everything on earth. You've been asked a very important question, Cozzy — THE question, the most important question ever asked. And the voice won't stop until you give it an answer."

*Oh really? And what question is that?*

"Do you want the world to end?"

Cozzy blinked hard and shook the water from her sopping ears again. *What did you just say?* she asked.

But the old man had vanished.

Since she knew she'd never be able to get back to sleep after such a bizarre and unsettling experience (and she was already drenched, anyhow), Cozzy decided to go in search of breakfast. One thing about rainstorms — while they inevitably soaked you, they also provided strays with their easiest source of fresh drinking water. Cozzy positioned her body atop a gutter grate — a trick she'd learned long ago, as the grate didn't allow for any puddles or pooling beneath her — and dropped her mouth into the small stream flowing alongside the curb, lapping herself a better drink than she'd had in days.

As she drank, Cozzy couldn't help but laugh to herself. Drinking water used to be so easy — walk up to your bowl, drink your thirst away, and if it dried up too soon, meow incessantly until someone refilled it for you. If that was too boring, just wait for the granddaughter to do the dinner dishes.

*"Jillian!" Grammy yelled. "Why do you insist on letting her do that? She has her own bowl, you know!"*

*"She likes it!"*

*Cozzy craned her neck around the neck of the faucet and lapped at the trickling water Jillian had set for her. While she knew it was the same water that waited for her in her bowl at all times, something just always seemed special about getting to drink straight from the tap. It was funny how it upset Grammy so much; seriously, what did she care?*

*"I know you just do that to extend your time doing the dishes so you don't have to dive into your homework yet!"*

*"Nuh-uh!" Jillian exclaimed, "It's not homework time yet! We still have to have dessert first!"*

*Cozzy arched her back and Jillian responded by scratching the base of her tail, just as she wanted. Cozzy continued to drink, contented in the knowledge that she had trained her family so well.*

*Papa stood up from his seat at the dinner table with an overfull grunt and an offer for his granddaughter. "Finish the dishes and I'll start scooping the ice cream. Deal?"*

*Mid-drink, Jillian scooped Cozzy into her arms, nestled her face into the scruffy back of the cat's neck, and then gently lowered her to the linoleum floor. Cozzy pretended to wail in protest; even though she'd been full for a solid thirty seconds, she couldn't let her family know that she wasn't deeply disappointed!*

*"I know Cozzy," Jillian whispered into her ear, "but I'll let you drink straight from the faucet again tomorrow night, I promise!"*

A car drove by, careening through a standing puddle far too fast, splashing a cascade of water across the entire sidewalk and anyone unlucky enough to be near the side of the road. Cozzy was the only one there; of course, it didn't really matter since she was already soaked to the bone.

The extra dousing was punctuated by the voice again. *"Your time has come! You must give me your answer!"*

*You know what? At least have the decency to let me get some breakfast first!*

Cozzy slinked her way through an empty gas station to a nearby shopping center that housed four different restaurants, all of whom kept their dumpsters tucked neatly away in the rear employee-and-deliveries-only parking lot behind the buildings. This was always her first stop for food each day. Sometimes Cozzy had to do things to eat that she wasn't proud of or happy about, but usually, four restaurants times three shifts equaled a lot of bags, and all it took was one sloppy twist-tie job or a well-placed claw swipe to turn an overstuffed dumpster into a buffet. This morning was no exception, and the food was still relatively fresh by garbage standards.

"Do you even remember what kibbles taste like, Cozzy?"

Her head snapped up from the chicken carcass she was munching. It was the old man again.

*If you're asking me that, you already know the answer.*

"Just how long has it been?"

*I'm not sure. I've never been great at keeping time. Maybe two years? I know I've been out here through two winters on my own.*

"I'm sorry about what happened to your family."

*People die. That's what they do. I've come to accept it.*

"That's true," the old man agreed, "everyone dies. Not just people — cats, dogs, fish, trees — all life, eventually, dies. But you, Cozzy, you get to decide if that day is today."

*I still don't get what you're talking about.*

"I know you've heard the question. That's why I'm here. That's how this has always worked — you get the question, I show up to explain the situation, and when you're ready, you make your decision."

Her chicken bones picked clean, Cozzy turned her attention to what appeared to be the discarded end of a serving of meatloaf. This bag had turned out to be quite a score and Cozzy knew it was best to eat as much as she could before one of the owners discovered her and chased her away.

*Actually, I've just heard the demand for an answer,* she corrected. *But you're telling me the question is 'do I want the world to end?'*

"Yes."

Cozzy sat silently, not eating, not moving, and barely breathing.

"Yes," the old man repeated.

*So I decide I want the world to end, and …*

"And that's it," he finished for her. "The end of everything, all of it, in the blink of an eye. The Apocalypse, Armageddon, Ragnarok, or whatever you want to call it — the end of all life on earth. Because you say so."

*But…why?*

"Because that's the way it's always been," the old man said, "since the first cats joined the first humans down here. That's always been your place and your role. Some cultures almost got it right, like the Egyptians; they worshipped you as gods because they recognized a link between felines and the afterlife. The truth is this world's fate has always lain with you."

*Yeah, but why me? Why not a lion, or a tiger, or a house cat that, you know, actually has a house? Why do I have to take a break from sifting through garbage to decide the fate of the world?*

The old man shrugged. "Because your great-great-great-great … aw to heck with it, I have no clue how many generations back it goes! Because you're descended from the first who was asked, Cozzy. It's in your blood."

*Yeah, well, I'm still not sure you're asking the right cat …* Cozzy began to answer, looking up from her piece of meatloaf for the first time in minutes, but he was gone again.

Suddenly, a sound like a gunshot exploded just behind her head. Cozzy shot straight up into the air before seeing one of the restaurant owners with rocks in his hand. His first shot had barely missed her and had crashed into the side of the metal dumpster. Cozzy tore off as soon as her paws touched the wet pavement and before he could aim another throw.

It hadn't always been like this for Cozzy. For a long time life was good…very, very good. As good as it could be, actually.

Grammy and Papa had adopted Cozzy from the local shelter the day she was weaned, which also happened to be Jillian's fourth birthday. All Jillian wanted more than anything else that year was a kitten, but her and her mom's apartment wouldn't allow pets (how absurd!). However, there were no such silly rules at Grammy and Papa's house, and since Jillian's mom worked third shift at the hospital and she spent most evenings at her grandparents', Cozzy very quickly became *their* cat (all three of them). It was the precocious Jillian who'd named Cozzy, and though her name didn't make much sense for a female cat, she'd come to love and appreciate its quirkiness.

As Cozzy had told the old man, she was never good at keeping track of time, but she guessed she'd lived in the comfort and love of her family for at least a decade. Jillian had certainly grown up a lot, and not just physically (but darn if she hadn't gotten *so* much taller!). Again, silly, stupid, arbitrary rules had kept Cozzy from attending her dance recitals and school plays, and even her middle school graduation, but she always felt as if she was there and a part of Jillian's accomplishments, because she'd watched her practice and rehearse so often in the living room (not to mention she'd always, *always* sneak into the celebration photos afterwards!).

It was around that time Papa started getting sick. Cozzy was the first to realize it, though she didn't know just how sick he would get. She sensed enough to spend as much time as she could curled at Papa's feet at the end of the couch, then at the end of he and Grammy's bed, and then finally at the end of the special mechanical adjustable bed the nurses brought in. She honestly didn't realize just how sick he was until he stayed home with her and watched Jillian's eighth-grade graduation from his laptop.

No one needed to tell Cozzy when Papa passed away; she'd had dozed off on the couch and was awakened by the sound of Grammy crying at the kitchen table. No one else was there yet, although Cozzy knew that Jillian and her mom would come crashing through the door at any moment and wrap their arms around her. Still, until they got there, Cozzy nuzzled her face against Grammy's shin and rubbed herself back and forth against her legs. Almost instinctively, Grammy dropped a hand away from her eyes and stroked her fingers back and forth across Cozzy's arched spine. Cozzy knew it wasn't as good as one of her granddaughter's hugs, but she knew Grammy understood and appreciated it; after all, they were family.

Again, Cozzy was never good at telling time (she never understood why Grammy and Papa insisted that "the middle of the night" was no time to go outside), but she did understand that Papa had been sick for a long time before he passed, because she could feel a sense of relief from the rest of her family. "He's finally at peace," she overheard them say. "He's in a better place now." They were all horribly sad, but there was an odd comfort and calm that blanketed her family.

Things were very different with Grammy.

It sure didn't seem like it was that long since they'd lost Papa. It seemed like less time had passed than she'd been out on her own, but then again, Cozzy recognized how slowly her time as a stray had dragged along.

One night, just like every other night, Grammy had put down fresh kibbles and water for her, put a load of wash into the dryer, turned on the late news, and tucked herself into bed. Only she didn't wake up in the morning; in fact, she never woke up. Cozzy had meowed and meowed at her and even batted the edge of her blanket the way she knew Grammy *hated*, but she couldn't rouse her. That was how the nice lady next-door, who visited every morning for coffee and used to carpool to choir practice with Grammy, found them.

It just didn't make sense. Papa had been sick, but Grammy had been fine. From her hiding spot under the dresser Cozzy heard one of the paramedics say "her heart gave out" when speaking with the neighbor, but again, it didn't make sense. After all, Grammy's heart had been fine! She still loved Cozzy, Jillian, and everyone the same as always! There was no sense of calm this time, no sense of relief. Just rage. Rage and fear...sensible fear. The house was empty. Cozzy couldn't stay there on her own, and Jillian's and her mom's apartment wouldn't allow her. She knew the next words out of the paramedic's mouth after he saw her food and water bowls would be, "Call the shelter."

But he had left the screen door propped open. She darted through it in a flash, leaped down her front steps without even touching a single one, and scrambled away as quickly as her four legs could carry her.

*"YOUR TIME HAS COME! YOU MUST GIVE ME YOUR ANSWER!"*

*I know!* Cozzy thought, as loudly as she could.

*"YOUR TIME HAS COME! YOU MUST GIVE ME YOUR ANSWER!"*

*I said I know! I heard you the first dozen times! Geez!*

Cozzy took the long way to the park in case the rock-throwing restaurateur had decided to follow her (one could never be too careful). The voice boomed repeatedly inside her head the whole way, and apparently, it was becoming impatient. Rather than head directly back to the unfinished construction site, she meandered along the outskirts of the playground. On nice days when she was up for it, Cozzy sometimes stole beneath the tall hedges that framed the area and watched the kids play.

*It's abandoned today because of the rain,* she explained to the old man.

He chuckled. "You knew I was here this time!"

*I could sense you. You don't survive out here as long as I have if you allow anyone or anything to sneak up on you. Plus, I figured you were due to come back since the voice won't shut up.*

"I know it's not my place to ask, but are you any closer to making your decision?"

*As close as I was the first time I heard the question.*

"I'm sorry you're stuck with this responsibility, Cozzy," the old man said. "It's a heck of a spot. It's not a fair position to put you in."

Cozzy glared at the old man through the dripping rain from the bush fronds. *Fair?* she asked, incredulously. *You don't have to talk to me about fair. It wasn't fair to watch Papa suffer like he did. It wasn't fair to have the night steal Grammy from us like some cowardly thief. They were good people. They were my people, and I was their cat, and we were a family, and now ...*

Cozzy's indignation simply wore out. She turned her eyes to the merry-go-round.

*There are usually kids here to watch,* she explained again. *Families. But not today. It's raining today, and I can sense it'll be snowing again soon. And I don't know how much more of this I can take. And you, or whoever or whatever, is asking me if I want all of this to keep going?*

The old man let her words hang in the air, like the suspended drops of rain that paused on the shrub before finding their way to Cozzy's tired, threadbare coat. Finally, she looked up at him through wet eyes with what she realized was her last breath of indignation.

*Life isn't fair,* she told him. *Why should death be?*

The voice had gone quiet, which after a day of persistent shouting was more unsettling than being yelled at. It also, somehow, in a way she didn't understand, let Cozzy know it was time.

She had made her way back to her refuge of the aluminum siding tube and tucked herself away from the rain's assault, but somehow, in a way she didn't understand, she understood that wasn't right. The voice had gone silent as soon as she'd taken shelter. She knew that actions and words had meanings beyond themselves. She couldn't do this hiding within abandoned construction equipment.

Cozzy took a deep breath, pushed herself from her hiding spot into the driving rain, and with all the strength and little majesty she had left, she jumped atop the empty tube and closed her eyes. As soon as she did, the voice returned.

*"YOUR TIME HAS COME! YOU MUST GIVE ME YOUR ANSWER!"*

*I know,* Cozzy thought, much differently this time.

*"YOUR TIME HAS COME! YOU MUST GIVE ME YOUR ANSWER!"* it demanded.

*No.*

*"YOUR TIME HAS COME! YOU MUST GIVE ME YOUR ANSWER!"* the voice repeated.

Cozzy opened her eyes and looked straight up into the blinding storm. *You're not listening to me.* She steeled herself. *My answer is no. No, I do not want the world to end.*

*"WHY?"* the voice bellowed.

*No one said I had to give an explanation,* Cozzy defiantly spat back against the rain.

*"WHY?"* the voice bellowed again.

*Who cares?* Cozzy screamed to herself and to whoever or whatever was listening. *The why doesn't matter!*

*"WHY?"* the voice insisted.

*THIS IS WHY!* Cozzy's mind screamed. She closed her eyes and let the memory overflow her more than the downpour …

*A few days before Papa had passed, they were all in his bedroom with him — Grammy, Jillian, Jillian's mom, and Cozzy, curled at Papa's feet as always. Her whole family had tears in their eyes, although they weren't really crying. If there was such a thing as being so happy and so sad at the same time, that's what they were. Papa had a huge smile on his face, and he reached out and took his granddaughter's hand. He'd been somewhat loopy for a while and half-asleep even when his eyes were open, but on this night, with them, he was all there.*

*"This world is yours, Jillian," he told her. "It's all yours. It was made for you. You are so brave, and so strong, and you make me so proud! There is nothing you can't do, so don't you ever let anyone tell you any differently. Go out there and grab it. Reach for the stars, because they're yours for the taking."*

*This world isn't mine to end,* Cozzy thought, her eyes clenched. *It belongs to Jillian, and all the granddaughters and grandsons. And I would never turn a good man like Papa into a liar.*

Cozzy didn't open her eyes until she noticed that the wetness on the back of her neck felt different. It wasn't the teeming rain anymore; it was a soothing, slightly rough, but entirely caring feeling that she hadn't experienced in years. She couldn't place the physical sensation, but she felt something else as well ... something more important, something more powerful, and something else she hadn't felt in a long, long time.

She felt safe. And loved.

Cozzy opened her eyes, and to her shock and panic, they were completely out of focus, so much that she couldn't see. Frantically, she blinked repeatedly, trying to regain all her senses at once.

Before she could see clearly, something deep inside of Cozzy suddenly recognized the sensation against the back of her neck — it was another cat's tongue. Her mother was bathing her. As soon as she realized that, her eyesight cleared.

She looked directly up and into a face that she hadn't seen in years. Her features had aged and she was an adult, but it wouldn't matter if twenty years or two thousand years had passed — Cozzy would always, *always* instantly recognize that face.

It was Jillian.

Jillian's eyes welled and her hands flew to her mouth. A handsome man who radiated kindness stood beside her and wrapped his arm around her shoulder.

"What is it, sweetheart?" he asked.

"The kitten," she whispered. "The first of the litter ... it looks just like Cozzy!"

"Cozzy?" a young, excited voice asked. "Who's Cozzy?"

Jillian took the hand of the young woman who'd piped up. "Cozzy was Grammy and Papa and my cat when I was your age!"

"Grammy doesn't have a cat!" another young voice declared.

"No," the kind man explained, "not Grammy Sara. Your mom's Grammy and Papa. Grammy Sara's parents."

"Oh, the one's we're named after?" the boy asked again.

Jillian beamed at him. "That's right Bobby. The Grammy and Papa you and your sister are named after. We looked everywhere for Cozzy after Grammy passed away, but we could never find her."

The young girl wrapped her arms around her mom's waist, and her father tousled her hair. "Well Wonder-Twins," he declared, "I think we know which kitten of Angel's litter is going to join our family! Agreed?"

Mary looked up at her mom. "Can we name her Cozzy, too?"

Jillian beamed, and struggle as she might to stay awake, a yawn overwhelmed Cozzy. As she drifted off to sleep nestled against her mother's body, she heard Jillian say, "Sure! Although we don't even know if that kitten is a boy or a girl yet! But geez, wouldn't it be funny to stick *another* little girl kitty with that name?"

It seemed much later when Cozzy awoke; she'd been through so much she doubted she'd ever be able to explain, and yet still, she had no clue how much time had elapsed. There were a number of other kittens squeezed into the plush, towel-lined box with her and her mother, all of them asleep. When she looked up this time, the only face she saw was that of the old man.

"I'm proud of you, Cozzy," he told her. "You did good. Not that any of us ever doubted."

*Where am I?* she asked.

"Your next life!" he said. "What, you can accept all those ghost stories you heard over the years, but it's too hard to believe that cats actually *do* get nine lives?"

*You mean...?*

"Look Cozzy, I'd be lying if I said I understood all of this, and I've been around a *lot* longer than you! Like I told you, this is how it works. At the end of each of your lives, you decide whether or not the world ends. You say no, the world goes on and you come back again. Then, after nine times, you pass the torch to the next cat in line. I'd tell you more about what awaits you after that, but that's a surprise I refuse to ruin...nor do I have the words to properly describe it!"

*How did you know I'd say no?* Cozzy asked. *I mean, after everything, how did you know?*

The old man smiled at her, genuinely and proudly. "You cats! You're stubborn, pig-headed, independent, opinionated, and it's not in your blood to quit, no matter what ... just like humans. That's why you get asked the question."

*Will I ... will I remember all of this?* Cozzy asked.

"Nah," the old man replied. "You couldn't fully enjoy this life if you did. And if any cat ever deserved to enjoy her next life, it's you."

Cozzy started to nod off again, but she shook her new small head violently to stay awake for another moment. *Wait, don't go yet!* her mind screamed. *I have one more question!*

"What is it, Cozzy?"

*How did I ... before I forget, how did I end up here? With Jillian again?*

144

The old man smiled as another colossal yawn pushed the kitten towards sleep. "It is highly unusual," he admitted. "Normally, there's a much longer gap between lives than this, but this opportunity presented itself and whoever or whatever is in charge decided reuniting you and Jillian was too good to pass up. That you deserved it … both of you."

Cozzy yawned again as sleep began to overtake her. The old man reached out a hand that wasn't really there, and gently pressed it against the top of her tired head as she drifted off.

"Not everything is unfair," he told her.

**MATT BECHTEL** was born just south of Detroit, Michigan (cursing him a Lions fan), into a mostly-Irish family of dreamers and writers as opposed to the pharmaceutical or construction giants that share his surname. As such, he has spent most of his years making questionable life decisions and enjoying the results. Mentored by their late-founder Bob Booth, he serves on both the Executive Committee of the Northeastern Writers' Convention (a.k.a. Camp Necon) and as a partner in the Necon E-Books digital publishing company. His writing tends towards dark humor / satire and has been compared to Ray Bradbury and Cormac McCarthy. He currently lives in Providence, Rhode Island (and if you look closely at his author's picture you can see that he follows Irish tradition and signs his initials into the head of his Guinness).

Please visit Matt online at http://www.mattbechtel.com/
https://www.facebook.com/mattbechtel
Twitter: @mattbechtel

Made in the USA
Las Vegas, NV
16 July 2021